CW00959640

The Tallyman

THE TALLYMAN

Bill Knox

Constable • London

Constable & Robinson Ltd
3 The Lanchesters
162 Fulham Palace Road
London W6 9ER
www.constablerobinson.com

First published in Great Britain 1968
This edition published in Great Britain by Constable,
an imprint of Constable & Robinson Ltd 2004

A copy of the British Library Cataloguing in
Publication Data is available from the British Library

ISBN 1-84119-943-5

Printed and bound in the EU

Chapter One

It was a grey Monday afternoon in mid-January with a hint of snow on a keen northeast wind. And it would soon be dusk. Already the first street lamps had begun to glitter beside the River Clyde. Other lights burned bright inside the squat Greek-Doric bulk of Glasgow's Justiciary Building, a signal that the High Court was in session.

The man in the dock in the north courtroom wore a faded but neatly pressed blue suit which he'd tugged carefully at the knees before sitting between the police escort. The jury box was empty.

Andrew Fergan had pleaded guilty to murder. For the Crown, the Advocate Depute uttered little more than a dozen words in moving for sentence. Fergan's counsel, unusually embarrassed, managed to beat even that record for brevity by announcing his client wished nothing said on his behalf.

So now the rest was for Lord Mains as presiding judge. Almost the only sound in the broad, chill courtroom was an occasional rustle as that wizened, monkeylike figure, his robes of white and scarlet a vivid splash of colour against the dark mahogany panelling, studied the papers spread before him.

'A dull day for the fans of justice,' murmured the round-faced out-of-town pathologist, slumped hands in pockets in the front row of the official seating. 'Just as well they didn't pay to get in – they'd be wanting their money back by now.' He jerked his head a fraction towards the man in the dock. 'This one is yours, isn't he?'

'My division. I only mopped up at the edges.' Detective Chief Inspector Colin Thane, head of Glasgow's Millside Division Criminal Investigation Department, hunched himself forward a little. 'He made it easy enough for us.'

'So I heard.' The pathologist was tempted to follow up the opening. But something in Thane's face decided him against it. 'Well, the rest of it shouldn't take long.'

Thane nodded. Andrew Fergan could hardly be accused of wasting the court's time. Thirty-one, medium height, with dark, thinning hair, he'd been brought up from the cells only three minutes ago.

The charge had been read aloud by the clerk of court . . . 'that you did, on the public footpath outside the licensed premises known as the Turkish Raven in King Street, Glasgow, present a loaded revolver at John Laverick, discharge the said revolver, fatally wound the said Laverick, and did thus murder him.'

Andrew Fergan had shown no more than passing interest.

Almost unconsciously, Colin Thane let one hand slide inside his jacket and touch the letter there. His mouth tightened. The letter had arrived by first post that morning. At any time it would have posed a temptation. On this particular day it amounted to something resembling the answer to a prayer.

On the bench, Lord Mains set aside the last of the papers, sat back, and cleared his throat.

'Andrew Fergan . . .'

Nudged by the constable on his right, Fergan rose. His knuckles rested lightly on the wooden rail which ran along the top of the dock.

'Fergan, you have pleaded guilty to a charge of murder. The wilful and deliberate taking of human life must bring its full punishment, and the duty of this court is clear.' The thin, precise voice paused. 'I sentence you to imprisonment for life.'

There were the inevitable gasps from the public area. But Andrew Fergan's expression didn't change. He nodded, turned slowly, met Thane's gaze, looked past him, and gave a faint grimace. Then he headed down the stairway at the rear of the dock, the stairway which led back to the cells.

A heavy door slammed shut. For once, the sound made Thane wince.

An incipient buzz of conversation died beneath an icy glare from the bench. Lord Mains wrote quickly on a scrap of paper, passed the note down to the clerk, then pushed back his chair.

An usher bellowed. The court rose with a quick scuffle of feet.

Moving with the dignity only a man small in stature can achieve, Lord Mains left the bench and disappeared towards the judges' room.

'Coffee break.' The pathologist snorted his disgust. 'Well, I won't make that witness box today, that's for sure.' He glanced at his watch. 'Still, I suppose I'd better hang on.'

'Uh-huh.' Thane answered absently, looking round. The clerk was in a low-voiced conversation with the Advocate Depute and Fergan's counsel. The latter, frowning a little, seemed inclined to argue. But Thane was more concerned with the emptying public benches. He saw a face he'd expected, drew a deep breath, and set off in pursuit.

He caught up just outside the courtroom, in the main entrance hall of antiseptically clean black-and-white marble.

'Mrs Fergan –'

The woman turned. Andrew Fergan's wife was in her late twenties, a small, plump, very ordinary brunette in a green tweed coat. She carried a pair of gloves as though no longer sure what to do with them, and her eyes had a dazed, faraway look. The middle-aged man by her side kept his hand on her arm, frowning.

'Mrs Fergan, I' – Thane searched for the words he needed and couldn't find them – 'I'm sorry. If you want to see him for a moment before he leaves –'

The older man cut him short. 'The lawyer said he'd arrange that, mister. We'll let him do something for his fee. Right, Irene?'

'I suppose so.' Her voice was low, forced. 'This is my father, Mr Thane.'

'Aye.' The man gave him a cold, fractional nod. 'So you're the one, eh? I suppose you did what you had to do. But you'd the wrong man in that dock. You know it.'

'I'm sorry.' Again that wasn't what he wanted to say. But it was the nearest he could get. 'Mrs Fergan, if you'd like a car to take you home afterwards –'

She shook her head. 'I don't think so.'

Father and daughter moved off. Thane shrugged, lit a cigarette, and stayed where he was.

Moving past in a flutter of black gown, an advocate saw him and waved a greeting. Thane acknowledged with a faintly weary grin.

Topping the six-foot mark, Millside's C.I.D. chief was the kind of man most people remembered. In his early forties, he had close-clipped dark hair and a face best classified as cheerfully rugged. Wearing a quiet Lovat tweed suit, he filled it in burly, athletic fashion, and when he moved, it was with the controlled, muscular ease of a man still in peak condition . . . even if he'd put on a few pounds since the days when he'd been an amateur heavyweight with the police boxing team.

A trio of Northern Division detectives were drifting in his direction. For once he didn't feel like company and headed out of the main door, on to the courthouse steps.

8

Next moment he wished he hadn't. A cold, knife-edged wind tugged at his clothes. An unending stream of traffic was growing along the busy Saltmarket, leaving a stink of exhaust fumes. On duty at the foot of the steps, a red-nosed constable shivered in the gloom.

Thane moved into the shelter of one of the tall stone portico pillars and leaned against it, drawing on his cigarette, trying to put Andrew Fergan's case out of his mind. He'd enough problems of his own.

But it wasn't easy. Fergan's case was the kind any cop with a conscience loathed, the kind where if any sympathies existed they lay with the killer. Still, it had been murder, a small battalion of psychiatrists had agreed on Fergan's sanity, and the rest was inevitable.

He dropped the cigarette and mashed it under heel, turning to his own dilemma, touching his jacket again to make sure the letter was still there.

What did you do when a city bank offered you twice your present take-home pay and a nine-till-five, five-day week as their security chief – with a guaranteed annual bonus thrown in?

Five thousand pounds a year . . .

He looked down again at the uniformed cop on the pavement. The man stood rubbing his hands together, lips moving silently in a way that didn't need a lip-reading expert.

What did you do? By police terms Thane knew he'd come pretty far and fairly fast. He was the youngest Glasgow C.I.D. man to have his own division. And his home life was settled enough – a wife he loved, two school-age youngsters, ten years to go on the house mortgage, three more payments due on the car.

He'd been lucky. But maybe this was luck again. Even if he reached top echelon at Headquarters he'd never equal the kind of money the bank job offered – offered now. And there was Mary to consider. She'd taken fifteen years of wondering whether he'd get home, of the telephone ringing in the middle of the night, of all the rest of it.

She'd like the bank job. Yet there was something odd, unreal about the idea of a nine-till-five routine, of weekends they could call their own, of all the rest.

It was going to take a lot of thought, and this was the wrong time. He moved away from the pillar, heading for the door again.

'Thane . . .'

The hoarse bellow brought him round, surprised. Puffing out of the darkness, coming fast up the steps, Detective Chief Superintendent William Ilford, head of the city's C.I.D., ignored the duty constable's salute and headed straight towards him.

'Came on over on foot.' The man his juniors called 'Buddha' Ilford showed little of his usual phlegmatic calm as he gasped for breath. 'Damned traffic – quicker this way.'

Thane nodded. Headquarters was only a long stone's throw away from the Justiciary Buildings. So, for that matter, was the City Mortuary. The wittier of Glasgow's layabout 'neds' had long ago christened the resultant triangle 'Happy Valley'.

'Something on, sir?' There had to be when Ilford hurried anywhere.

'Eh? Haven't they told you yet?' Ilford swallowed more air and glared his impatience. 'Lord Mains wants us – both of us and right now. What's been going on?'

'Nothing – at least nothing I know about.' Thane's mind raced over the possibilities. When one of Her Majesty's law lords issued a summons it usually meant trouble for all concerned. 'Didn't they tell you, sir?'

'No.' Ilford shouldered his bulky way through the courthouse door, Thane at his heels. 'All I got was a phone call telling me to get over.'

Following him across the inner hallway, conscious of

plenty of interested eyes, Thane cursed the notion which had taken him outside. 'There's been only one Millside case today –'

'Which?'

'Fergan, this afternoon. He got life.'

'Fergan.' Ilford made a noise like a groan. 'Well, if it's that kind of trouble we'll soon find out.' He pointed ahead.

A gowned and wigged trio were coming down the centre corridor which led to the judges' suite. The clerk of court was in the lead, his face brightening as he saw the two detectives. A few paces behind him, the Advocate Depute and Fergan's counsel followed at a slower pace. Fergan's counsel looked far from happy, and his Crown opposite number was frowning, scratching under his wig with the tip of a pencil.

'You've arrived, Chief Superintendent – good.' The clerk gave a faint sigh of relief, then glanced at Thane, his lips tightening a little. 'Mr Thane, I've been looking for you everywhere in the building, from the restaurant and the cells to – to the ruddy men's room.'

'I was outside –' began Thane.

'It doesn't matter.' The clerk broke off to give a sudden, forced smile as the two counsels passed. They returned the farewell in equally seedy fashion. Then he got back to business. 'Lord Mains is waiting. If you'll come with me –'

'What's on?' demanded Ilford. 'Man, you're throwing us in like ruddy ewe-lambs.'

'To a slaughter, Chief Superintendent?' The clerk sniffed a little. 'Then please don't bleed on the judge's rug. We had it cleaned for Christmas.'

Buddha Ilford growled, but the clerk was already on his way. They went after him, past an elaborate series of friezes depicting Athenian justice, through a set of swing doors into what was normally forbidden territory, and finally stopped outside another door.

11

The clerk knocked and a voice answered. He opened the door and waved them through but didn't follow. As the door closed again, a sneeze rang out.

'Damn the draught in that courtroom,' complained Lord Mains peevishly. 'Someone's going to die of pneumonia on that bench.'

He blew his nose on a large white handkerchief. The sound had a two-tone trumpet effect. Thane fought down a grin as he looked at the thin, wrinkle-faced little man who was among the most senior of Her Majesty's justices for Scotland.

Lord Mains had left his robes and wig on a coatstand in one corner of the room and stood with his back to a blazing coal fire which supplemented the regular heating. Bald, with a vague tonsure of pepper-and-salt hair, a plain dark suit, starched white wing collar and white cravat gave him the appearance of a Dickensian clerk. Sharp, pale eyes inspected them with unhurried deliberation.

He sniffed and returned the handkerchief to its pocket.

'Thank you for coming.' The voice was still peevish and dry. 'Ilford, I've seen your chief inspector in the witness box a few times, but we haven't met at closer range.'

'Sorry.' Quickly, Ilford made the introductions.

It was, decided Thane, like shaking hands with a claw. And he wondered just how old the man was – certainly old enough to be drawing a pension in any other profession.

'Well, sit down.' Lord Mains removed himself reluctantly from the coal fire and took to a deep armchair. A tray with a coffeepot and a used cup lay nearby. He waited till they were settled in other chairs then scowled a little. 'I want to talk about Andrew Fergan.'

'I thought –' began Ilford.

A thin finger stabbed for silence. 'For the moment, I'd prefer to perform that exercise, Ilford. However, I seem to remember you smoke a pipe. And I seem to have left my tobacco at home . . .'

Chief Superintendent Ilford quickly levered himself up and passed over his pouch. Lord Mains smelled the contents carefully, pursed his lips a little, then began to pack a battered briar pipe. It had a bowl which seemed big enough to take an ounce at a filling.

When he'd finished, he handed the pouch back and struck a match. He wasn't satisfied until the briar was going like a tar-boiler's chimney.

'Reasonable,' he admitted. 'Now, about Fergan. I have already told the Advocate Depute and Fergan's counsel that in terms of law I have no criticism to make of the conduct of the case or the police information as presented.'

Thane began to draw a breath of relief, then stopped as those needle-sharp eyes glared from behind the cloud of pipe smoke.

'On the other hand, in my opinion – in my nonjudicial opinion – the situation is a damnable disgrace.' That thin forefinger stabbed again. 'Do you challenge that view, Chief Inspector?'

Slowly, Thane shook his head. Beside him, Ilford sat reddening a little, his mouth a tight line.

'Good. When one spends one's life hearing evidence allegedly given under oath, actual honesty becomes a rare and valued commodity,' said Lord Mains grimly. He got up, crossed to a small table, and lifted a sheaf of papers. 'Now, Andrew Fergan is, or was, an insurance clerk. He experimented in petty embezzlement from his firm, then had to find the money quickly. As a result, he borrowed the sum of one hundred pounds from an unlicensed money-lender. The police have a name for them. Ah –'

'Tallymen,' growled Ilford. 'Because they keep tally on what's owed – and the interest.'

'Quite.' Lord Mains gave a wintry smile. 'The interest

rates, I gather, are unusually well commensurate to risk?'

'Twenty to twenty-five per cent per week,' agreed Thane in a soft, bitter voice. 'The clients take the terms because they've no alternative. Banks wouldn't touch them. They're such poor risks that regular money-lenders would kick them downstairs.'

'Thank you. And repayment is rigorously enforced?' Lord Mains had his fingertips together, teacher taking pupil through a lesson they both knew backwards.

'Pay up and everything's fine,' nodded Thane. 'Fall behind, and the tallyman sends round a couple of heavies to jog your memory.'

'And if, like the unfortunate Fergan, you still can't pay?'

'Then the tallyman fixes a lower weekly figure. The interest keeps mounting, and the poor devil involved is on the hook till he dies,' said Thane, with a fair idea now what was coming.

'Exactly.' Lord Mains produced his handkerchief again, blew mightily, then leaned forward. 'According to the court reports this fellow Laverick was a known tallyman. He was outside that bar to collect payments. Isn't it odd no records, no payment sheet and very little money was found on his body?'

'They work in pairs,' grunted Ilford. 'The minder would grab the stuff. There's always a minder in the background on collection nights in case of trouble.'

'Or in case the tallyman is tempted to be unfaithful to his master?' queried the judge softly.

Ilford reddened even more, glanced at Thane, and gave a reluctant nod. 'Maybe.'

'Maybe.' Lord Mains repeated the word bleakly. 'Chief Superintendent, I have just sentenced a man to life imprisonment because he exterminated a parasite – a twenty-five-per-cent-per-week parasite who had driven him to

14

desperation.' He swung his attention back to Thane. 'But the parasite Laverick was only an agent for a larger parasite, correct?'

'That's how it looks, sir,' admitted Thane, smarting under the small man's icy disapproval. 'But –'

Lord Mains raised an eyebrow. ' "But," Chief Inspector? Are you seeking sympathy?'

'Hell, no!' Thane had had enough. 'Look, we turned over the whole damned division trying to find Laverick's minder. If anyone –'

Buddha Ilford had been hunched in his chair, scowling down at his navel in that studied contemplation which had earned the irreverent nickname. Now he cut Thane short with a warning growl, hoisting himself upright.

'Maybe it's better if I answer for my officers,' he said deliberately. 'Then there's less chance of – of a misunderstanding.'

Lord Mains nodded and took a long, slow puff at his pipe. 'Good tobacco, Chief Superintendent. Doesn't become too – ah – heated.'

'I like it that way.' Ilford forced a smile. 'On the tallymen, we've had problems all along. We've mopped up operators time after time. Usually we get enough to nail them for operating as unlicensed money-lenders. But anything more?' He rumbled his disgust. 'Witnesses won't back up an assault charge. They'll claim they fell out of bed, tripped over the dog, any idiot story they can dream up. So the tallyman ends up with a fine he can pay out of the petty cash.'

'But you know these men,' reminded the judge, frowning.

'We know most of them,' agreed Ilford. 'But we also know there's a new tallyman ring operating – and we just can't get a lead on who's at the top.' He shrugged. 'Even if we did, how much good would it do?'

For nearly a minute the judge sat silent, pipe in mouth.

Then, without warning, he laid it down, rose, crossed over to the window, and looked out. The view was into an empty central yard. The long-dead courthouse architects had wisely decided the citizens of Glasgow shouldn't have the opportunity of lobbing a brick – to name nothing more lethal – into some judicial lap.

'Ever since I was a young lawyer I've found it helps to think aloud,' he said softly, still with his back to them. 'You understand?'

Thane glanced at Buddha Ilford. The C.I.D. chief gave a swift shake of his head and they said nothing.

'Politicians make our laws, the courts merely interpret them,' mused Lord Mains with a dry cynicism. 'If occasionally the law appears an ass, then perhaps the reason is that our politicians are – ah – too much engaged in demonstrating their talents in noisy debate. But I accept your problems, Ilford. And as a much younger man, Thane must learn that irritation is not necessarily condemnation.'

Buddha Ilford cleared his throat in noisy agreement. The small elderly figure still stared out of the window.

'I am a traditionalist, gentlemen, at least where old ways still seem the best. Until not very long ago Scotland had a particularly civilized outlook towards any individual charged with murder. No plea of guilty was allowed. Such a charge had to be proved by proper presentation of evidence to a jury.

'Now? Today I had to sit silent while that poor wretch Fergan first pleaded guilty, then declined to make any statement. I was left like some Civil Service rubber stamp, passing the only sentence prescribed by law. And I do not like being a rubber stamp.'

Suddenly he left the window and went back to the crackling fire. Watching, Thane realized this was a tired man, a troubled man, a surprisingly human man.

Lord Mains slapped his hands lightly together. 'Lecture

16

over. But two things I will say. Life imprisonment is a flexible phrase. The discretion lies with the Crown authorities. Recently they were naïve enough to release a particularly vicious thug after a mere nine years. I have – ah – transmitted my view that on this basis Fergan's term should be no more than five years. He will not be told, of course. Not for a little while, at any rate.'

'Five years!' Colin Thane gave a quiet sigh of relief. 'That's –'

'A salve to several consciences?' The judge's mouth twisted a little. 'I'm still thinking aloud, you'll remember. My second thought is that it would be grossly wrong for one of Her Majesty's judges to advise the police of this city.

'But' – he let the word hang, and the pale eyes became colder – 'I imagine a considerable effort will be concentrated on these tallymen, with much more in mind than a mere appearance at some lower court. In turn, I can promise that if the High Court found such an individual before it, if a High Court jury in its wisdom found him guilty . . .' The hands came together again, this time hard, like a pistol shot.

Lord Mains glanced at his watch. They took their cue, said goodbye, and went towards the door. As they left, the judge was already reaching for his heavy silk robes.

Outside, Buddha Ilford stumped a few steps in silence, then stopped and swore.

'You know what the old devil's done, don't you?'

'For a start, he's eased things for Fergan.' Thane lit a cigarette with hands that shook just a little and took a long, thankful draw.

'Fergan?' The C.I.D. chief practically snarled the name. 'I'm not talking about Fergan. I'm talking about us.' He glared at a passing court official. The man blinked and quickened his stride.

17

'Well, he made it clear enough he wants a tallyman,' mused Thane.

'He wants one particular tallyman,' corrected Ilford heavily. 'He wants him tied up in a neat package, no messing about. He wants the big boy. And if we don't produce him, you can bet there's going to be twenty different types of backdoor hell to pay.'

Thane nodded. People were beginning to drift back through the main hallway and into the north courtroom. His own and Ilford's reappearance had been a signal for the court grapevine. The last of the coffee drinkers were returning.

'I'm giving *you* the job,' said Ilford suddenly.

'Me?' Thane wondered for a moment if he'd heard correctly. 'But this – this isn't a divisional job!'

'It's yours.' Ilford was unmoved. 'It blew up in Millside Division, so Millside is as good a place to start as any.' The C.I.D. chief dug his hands deep into his coat pockets. 'Thane, by next High Court either we've this boss tallyman on the indictment list or someone's head goes on the chopping block. Understand?'

'More or less . . . sir.'

'Right.' Ilford took out his pipe and pouch, saw how little tobacco was left, and swore again. 'Any notion where you'll start?'

'I've one or two possibles.' A stubborn instinct made Thane leave it at that.

'Oh?' Ilford waited, then shrugged. 'All right, it's your case. But keep in touch.' He growled to himself. 'Next stop off is to explain things to the Chief Constable. He knew I was called over – and he'll want to know why.'

He stumped off, a large, tweedy bear of a man carrying his own personal thundercloud.

So all Millside Division had to do was find the character who'd become known as The Tallyman. Something all

18

eight city divisions had been trying to accomplish for months.

Find him – and nail him.

Colin Thane grimaced. All he needed was a small miracle. And miracles were usually in short supply in Millside's grimy sprawl.

He tapped his chest to make sure the bank-job letter was still there. Hell, you didn't get your shoes muddy working in a bank. They brought you tea, they called you 'mister' – and the customers usually had a bath at least once a week.

Life would be peaceful as a security man. Maybe he'd even find time to paint the kitchen for Mary.

After he'd nailed The Tallyman.

He still owed that much to Andrew Fergan.

Chapter Two

Once upon a time someone took a city map, a ruler and a newly sharpened pencil and drew the arbitrary lines which chopped Glasgow's urban sprawl into a series of apparently neat police divisions.

He's been cursed ever since, nowhere with better reason than in Millside Division. An oblong slab of the northwest area, Millside seemed to incorporate a little bit of everything that could possibly spell trouble.

It had dockland and rat-infested slums along the Clyde, backed by dark, grim factories, more tenement buildings and occasional waste ground where demolition hammers had performed their acts of mercy. Further out, a thin fringe of suburban bungalows had once been on the edge of open country. Now they were overshadowed by multistorey low-rent council flats – and by new industrial plants where operatives wore white coats and complained about lack of car-park space.

Millside had the worst pockets of unemployed and unemployable, the highest welfare roll and some of the toughest hooligan 'neds' in the city. Just as it had some of the best-paid industrial workers, a Better Gardens League, and old ladies who kicked up hell if their street wasn't swept on schedule.

Sitting up front beside the uniformed driver in the C.I.D. duty car, Colin Thane watched the familiar street names slide by. Neon shop-signs glared down on the evening rush-hour traffic, there were queues at the bus stops and the beginnings of other queues outside some of the bingo halls.

He sat silent, listening to the crackling radio. Headquarters Control was trying to sort out a multiple crash just south of the river – and he could imagine the confusion that was causing to cross-town traffic.

'Sir' – the driver, a large, slow-spoken individual named Erickson, glanced briefly in his direction – 'will we be on that warehouse job again tonight?'

'Not if there's anything better to do,' Thane told him dryly. The tip that the Alhambra Storage warehouse would be burgled, the target a consignment of imported transistor radios, had come in over a week ago. He'd had a watch kept on it ever since, with the net result the near arrest of a detective by an uninformed branch car answering a report of a 'suspicious character' hanging around.

Erickson grunted hopefully. A moment later he flicked the turn indicator and the car swung off the main road.

Millside police station lay halfway down the side street, a Gothic stone structure with bits and pieces added. Thane left the car at the station's main door, watched it purr off towards the garage yard, then went into the warmth of the brightly lit building.

They were dealing with what looked like the results of a husband-and-wife punch-up at the inquiry counter. Thane winked at the sergeant on duty over the couple's heads and climbed the stairway to C.I.D. territory. In the main C.I.D. room, a scatter of desks, telephones and filing cabinets, things seemed fairly quiet. He exchanged a greeting with a couple of newly arrived night-shift men and went through into his own office.

As he'd expected, it already had an occupant. Standing beside the divisional map which occupied most of one wall, Detective Inspector Phil Moss had an assortment of colourheaded pins held between his lips and was adding them one by one to the crime locations already studding the tracery of streets.

'Mmph,' said Moss, still concentrating on his task.

'Someday you're going to swallow those things – and stationery department won't like it,' warned Thane, tossing his hat on the desk and shrugging out of his overcoat. 'Much been happening?'

Moss pressed one more pin into place and spat the rest from mouth to hand. 'Dull as a graveyard – so far, anyway.' The small, lean figure thumbed almost despondently towards the map. 'That thing's a week out of date. And I took a look through the pending file. There are two Headquarters requests which –'

'Which can wait till we're good and ready.' Thane moved round his desk, slumped into the worn leather chair he'd inherited from his predecessor, and shook his head. 'Phil, one of these days they'll want to know how often we change our socks.' He pressed the intercom buzzer, waited, and heard the orderly's voice answer. 'Any tea out there? Two if you can – one for Inspector Moss, weak as it comes.'

When he released the switch he found Moss watching him, and knew why.

'He got life, Phil.'

Moss nodded. 'And you got the judge's carpet,' he said dryly. 'At least, that's the word I got – one of the Central Division boys was on the phone. Was it rough?'

'He didn't pat us on the back,' said Thane wryly.

'Aye.' There was sardonic sympathy in the grunt, then Moss perched himself on the edge of the desk, waiting.

A small, grey, shabbily dressed man with sparse, sandy hair, the Millside C.I.D. second-in-command was in his mid-fifties. Shirt cuffs frayed, blue suit almost past the stage of being pressed and cleaned again, he was a bachelor who was the constant despair of the hopeful widow who ran the boarding-house he called home.

Once, when he'd been walking along Main Street, an elderly woman had pressed money into his hand and had told him to buy a good meal.

It hadn't worried Moss. Nothing really did for long – except perhaps the state of the stomach ulcer he'd cherished for almost ten years. That ulcer was the day-to-day barometer of his outlook, a barometer famed throughout the city's divisional offices.

But the chuckles still held plenty of respect. An underlying, long-term friendship was only part of the reason why Thane and Moss formed a particularly efficient team.

'Phil' – Thane leaned forward on one elbow, trying to keep his manner easy – 'we've been handed a sizeable headache. We've to nail the big fellow in the tallyman setup.'

'Or else?' Moss raised an eyebrow.

Thane grimaced. 'Use your imagination. Now listen.'

He told the story. Moss sat where he was, nodding occasionally, already assessing what they were being asked to achieve.

It was in this type of situation that Thane came nearest to envying him. Phil Moss could tackle the most tedious research job, analyse anything from a company report to an old income-tax return, sift through a mountain of detail – and be happily in his element.

Thane was very different and knew it. While he'd learned the rules and tried to work by them, there would sometimes come a situation when he had a hunch and little else . . . and he'd throw caution aside, charge on in, then sweat out the results.

That was when Moss most often came to the rescue. Dry, complaining, insolent, he could still magic up a way which gave a second chance. Just as, by nudging Thane every now and again, he managed to prevent the divisional paperwork from reaching shambles proportions.

They formed an odd partnership – Thane from the regional crime squad, Moss from a one-time Headquarters desk. But it worked.

Or it usually did.

As Thane finished, the orderly knocked on the door and came in. A fresh-faced police cadet who shaved once a week more from pride than necessity, he laid down two chipped cups on a tin tray.

'Anything else, sir?'

Thane shook his head. The orderly went out and, as the door closed again, Moss lifted the nearest cup.

'Where do we start, then?'

'I'm hoping we've started.'

'That picture stunt?' Moss sipped, scowled, and gave his cup a brief stir with a pencil. 'When should we get them?'

'This evening sometime. As soon as the prints are ready.' When he'd made the arrangement, Thane's own motives had been uncertain. But Millside Division had a convenient love-hate relationship with the *Evening Bugle* and in particular with the *Bugle's* crime man, Jock Mills. Crime reporters believed in storing up goodwill, and when Millside asked a favour it could usually be arranged.

There were always a reasonable number of press photographers on duty outside the High Court. One had been at work all that day, shooting a lot of film, concentrating on anyone entering or leaving the court's public entrance.

'Aye. We may know someone.' Moss was hardly enthusiastic. 'Then there's always Fergan's case file –'

'Which we know by heart.' It was Thane's turn to be unenthusiastic.

Fergan's file was thick enough, but the final story pathetically thin.

He'd backed too many losers while the household bills mounted up. His wife didn't know what was happening until the grocery store stopped delivering on credit, but other people did – particularly the bookies, who wanted their money.

So the insurance clerk studied form until he lined up a horse which seemed a long-odds certainty. Then he dipped the firm's till for a fifty-pound cash bet.

Whatever happened to the horse, it staggered in last but one. He had to replace the cash in a hurry, he couldn't tell his wife, his friends had had enough, even the neighbourhood money-lenders had got the word.

The tallyman remained. Fergan got his fifty pounds and another fifty to fend off the angrier creditors. No contract, no signatures, just cash in his pocket and a breathing space – at twenty-five per cent per week, compound.

By the end of the first month the hundred had become two hundred. After three months, even with a few struggling repayments, he owed over five hundred.

Andrew Fergan loaded the revolver he'd brought back as a souvenir from the Korean War. He put three bullets into John Laverick, then tried to shoot himself. The gun jammed, and he hadn't the courage to try again. So he found a telephone box, called the police, then went back and waited beside the body.

'There's the way they make initial contact,' mused Moss. He shook his head at Thane's offered cigarettes, dipped into a baggy pocket, and produced a plain, unbranded pack.

'What we know about initial contact could go on a ruddy postcard.' Thane glared at his second-in-command's choice of smoke. 'Those things again?'

'They're doing me good.' Moss lit up with a dogged determination. The herbal mixture burned like a scrap-tyre dump. 'Look, the idea is they stimulate the stomach juices while they –'

'While they kill off the rest of humanity?' Thane's nostrils twitched in disgust. 'All right, let's talk about initial contact. Fergan could name a score of people who knew he

25

was getting desperate. Most of them admitted they'd mentioned it somewhere. Then Laverick telephones out of the blue, they meet in a bar – and that's it.' He took a gulp of tea and sighed. 'Laverick, just Laverick – even when The Tallyman put on pressure, it was through Laverick.'

Moss nodded. Laverick had been a small-time thug who'd graduated to clean shirts and polished shoes. But there'd been no lead back from him – not even a hint of who'd gone around with him as background minder.

'Then Fergan's family –'

'They didn't know anything.' Thane rubbed a hand across his forehead. 'No, we want a new approach. We want to organize ourselves another Fergan.'

'Set up a fake pigeon?' Moss was uncertain. 'It would take time, Colin. Then it would need luck –'

'There's the genuine variety,' mused Thane.

'And how do we find one?' queried Moss cynically. 'Advertise somewhere? "If your mammy doesn't know you've pawned the family silver, if you've just spent the works' holiday-fund money, the police would love to know –"'

'We'll see.' Thane wasn't prepared to argue. 'Anyway, stay here and take care of those photographs when they arrive. And there's one thing we can do. That bar, the Turkish Raven – it was always Laverick's collection point.'

'But The Tallyman would end that as soon as he heard what happened,' warned Moss. 'He'd switch to a new meeting place and get word round to the clients.'

'That's exactly what interests me,' Thane told him. 'It's been a couple of months since the shooting. All right, we couldn't find anyone at the time who'd admit to being one of Laverick's customers. But by now the regulars will have noticed who doesn't come around any more. Send Sergeant MacLeod along. He can hold his beer better than

26

most. And tell him to check back with you as soon as he's finished.'

'What about *you*?'

'Home first, then I'll try a couple of people on my own.' Thane drained the last of the tea, rose, and went for his hat and coat.

'But you'll be back?' queried Moss.

'Here?' Thane shook his head. 'Only if things really start happening. Bring the pictures out to my place around ten – I'll be finished by then.'

He was at the door when Moss remembered another problem.

'What about the Alhambra warehouse? Do we watch it again?'

'Leave it,' decided Thane. 'The men we save from there can tour around the division, usual places. I want the word spread we're looking for anyone who's on The Tallyman's hook – that maybe we can help them wriggle free.'

'Don't expect a queue at the door,' warned Moss.

'I only want *one*, Phil,' said Thane quietly.

He'd be lucky at that, he knew. But he was like a fisherman faced with a strange, mirror-calm pool. What he wanted was down there somewhere. He had to try a cast here and a cast there – keep trying, certain that sooner or later he'd see at least a ripple of truth.

Thane caught a bus out from town, got off near the end of his street, then walked down a long row of almost identical little bungalows to the one which was home.

The pavement was icy in patches and youngsters had built up a long, slippery slide. He steered round it and turned into his gateway. Still, he decided, winter had its compensations. For the moment, with the weeds underground, his garden looked no more unkempt than the rest.

The door opened before he could find his key. Mary had

been watching for him. She was dark-haired, with a smooth, fresh complexion and a figure which made nonsense of the fact she had two children of school age. And she was wearing a blue wool dress he'd always liked.

He kissed his wife in a way which made her raise a slightly quizzical eyebrow.

'What's *that* for?' she asked.

'General principle.' He shut the door, got rid of his hat and coat, and looked around. 'Where's everybody?'

'Fed and gone,' she said dryly. 'Tommy's got some Cub Scout test on, Jane's gone to watch TV at the Randolphs, and that good-for-nothing layabout you call a dog is sleeping on our bed.'

'Fine,' he said absently, then frowned. 'What's wrong with our own TV?'

'Nothing. But the Randolphs have a new colour set.'

'Oh.' Quickly, he changed the subject. 'Phil's coming round later, but I'll need to go out for a spell before then.'

'All right.' She smiled a little. 'Hungry?'

'Uh-huh.'

He followed her through to the front room, where the table was still set. Mary poured him a cup of tea, then headed for the kitchen and returned with his meal.

'Stew,' she said almost apologetically. 'And not so much cooked as cremated. The kids wanted theirs early.'

'It looks fine,' he said vaguely. In fact, it was only slightly singed at the edges and he tackled it with relish. Mary poured herself a fresh cup of tea, sat down opposite and watched in silence.

As he finished, she lit a cigarette and waited while he did the same.

'Now?' she queried.

'Now? Now what?'

'Now whatever's on your mind.' Her eyes crinkled.

28

'Colin, there are times when I can read you like the proverbial book. Do I get to be told or don't I?'

'Well' – he grinned sheepishly, took out the letter, and handed it over – 'this was in the morning post. I didn't open it till I got into the office.'

She unfolded the letter, frowned a little when she saw the bank's printed heading, then began reading. After a couple of paragraphs she stopped and looked up, excitement gathering.

'Colin –'

'Read it all,' he told her.

She did.

'What do you think?' he asked.

'It – it's wonderful!' Then, immediately, what he called her 'wife image' took control. 'But would you like to do it?'

'Swap thief-catching for a cushy nine-till-five security job and that kind of money?' His grin broadened. 'Why not?'

'They've a five-day week, pension scheme, executive dining room' – she looked up again from the letter, frowning a little – 'well, you'd need a new suit for a start.'

Thane chuckled. 'And the rest?'

'It – I don't know.' Carefully, she put the letter back in its envelope and handed it back. 'You'll go and see them?'

'Tomorrow morning. I phoned and made an appointment.'

'Does Phil or – or anyone else know?'

'Not yet.' He was puzzled. 'I thought you'd like the idea.'

'Like it?' She stared at him in astonishment. 'Colin, it's like a dream come to life – any cop's wife would feel that way!'

'The money's good,' he mused.

'Money?' She brushed the aspect aside. 'That's incidental. If – if –' she stopped short.

'If what?'

'If – if I thought you could be happy doing it,' she said slowly. 'That's what matters.' Then, quickly, practically. 'Well, you'll need your good suit tomorrow. I'll see if it needs pressing. And you'll wear that white shirt mother gave you at Christmas. And –'

'And that's enough for now.' He stubbed his cigarette, came around behind her, kissed her hair, and kept his hands on her shoulders for a moment. 'We'll see what they've got to say. All right if I take the car tonight?'

She nodded. 'You're going now?'

'Sooner I do, sooner I'll be back.'

When he left, Mary was clearing the table. If he'd seen her once the door closed, he'd have been even more bewildered.

She was crying.

Heading in towards town, fresh snow feathering the windscreen of his car, Colin Thane began planning as he went.

He'd told Moss there was no sense digging back into the Fergan file and he'd meant it. But there were two men who'd been minor, sideline characters in Fergan's case. They'd been questioned and the results had been pretty much a waste of time, yet maybe now they'd be worth trying again – trying for a different reason.

The first address was a tenement block near Main Street, just inside the Millside Division boundary. He parked, left the car, and didn't bother to lock up – Millside's car thieves usually went for a better class of vehicle than the Thane family's elderly, rusting Austin. A few paces away, above the nearest entry to the tall, dark building, a discreet red neon sign advised that 'Rab Hayes – Loans by Arrangement' was located three up.

Going through the tiled entry, Thane climbed the worn stone stairway past the private house doorways on each

30

landing. At last, he stopped outside a smaller version of the neon sign.

It was cold on the landing. He could feel the chill from the stone through his shoes as he rang the bell and looked up.

There was a glass transom above the door. He knew from his last visit that Hayes had a mirror fixed there, angled to give him a full-width view of the landing. Money-lenders were experts at the art of not taking chances.

A few moments passed, then locks clicked, the door opened and Hayes looked out. He was flabby, middle-aged and scowling. The heavy wool cardigan which flapped loose around him had a hole in one elbow, his sparse black hair was slicked back and there was whisky on his breath.

'Come in,' said Hayes shortly. 'It's not good for business having the police on the doorstep. That goes double after dark.'

As soon as he'd entered the hallway Hayes went through the ritual of relocking. Then he turned.

'It's official, I suppose – I mean, you're not here privately?'

'For a loan?' Thane grinned and shook his head.

'No harm asking.' Grumbling, the man led the way. The apartment was both business and living quarters. As they passed an opened door, Hayes thumbed towards an unmade bed. 'I was lying down. Toothache – hellish dose of it. Tried the old whisky cure, but it hasn't helped.'

Thane made a sympathetic noise as they went into the money-lender's office. It was a large room, with wall-to-wall carpet, a long, glass-topped desk and a couple of facing chairs which were simple enough to be expensive. The rest was filing cabinets and a small table with some potted cactus plants.

'I thought the Fergan business was over,' said Hayes,

gesturing towards the chairs and moving round behind the desk. 'I heard a radio bulletin say he got life.'

'He did.' Thane stayed on his feet and looked around. Rab Hayes wasn't big as money-lenders went, but he'd been in the business a long time and he'd learned along the way. The furnishings reeked discreet respectability. If there was a single discordant note – and it was probably deliberate – it was a calendar on one wall. It bore the information that it had been presented with the compliments of the Barbar Debt Recovery Agency. 'Let's say I'm tidying up the aftermath.'

'And I need tidying?' Hayes frowned, his small, shrewd eyes immediately hardening. 'If this has anything to do with my licence I want my lawyer around.'

'It's nothing like that,' Thane reassured him.

'Good.' Hayes relaxed a little. 'Chief Inspector, I run a straight business. People want money, I provide it. They pay me interest, sure – I'm not a charity. But it's fixed rate, a modest percentage and nothing more – with a signed agreement.' He spread his hands appealingly. 'Look, by the time I pay taxes and overheads I'd get a better return with my money in a bank account.'

Thane grinned. 'I'll weep for you later, Mr Hayes. Right now I want some help. Fergan came here looking for a loan and you chased him.'

'Correct.' The money-lender sucked expansively on his teeth and immediately winced. 'Damn that dentist – he told me I didn't need a filling.'

'We all make mistakes,' mused Thane.

'Huh. Well, I didn't with Fergan.' Hayes scowled down at his desk. 'I advertise loans up to five thousand, cash down, no security – but at my discretion. I talk to a client, man or woman. I size them up, make my own judgement. Fergan' – he shook his head – 'Fergan was trouble just looking for somewhere to happen. When I take on a client it's because I'm pretty sure I'll get my money back.'

'And sometimes that means outside help?' Thane thumbed towards the calendar.

'The Barbar service?' Hayes grinned and nodded. 'Now and again, if I've a problem. They're useful – and they stay well within the law.'

Thane nodded. Debt-recovery agencies were useful rather than popular. They collected bad debts, usually by arranged instalments of small, weekly sums, and charged commission on what they recovered for customers. The customers were as often as not shopkeepers. If there was pressure, it stayed at firm persuasion and the background threat of a court order. And he had heard of the Barbar agency more than once – it had several retired cops on staff, because of the built-in authority such men retained.

'You turned down Fergan,' he said again. 'You turn down others?'

'Every day.' The money-lender shrugged. 'It's part of the job. Chief Inspector, there isn't a hard-luck story variation I haven't heard. And I'm human – these people brush some of their misery off on me.'

'But you're not a charity,' murmured Thane. When it came down to basics, he reminded himself, there wasn't too much difference between Rab Hayes and the full-blown respectability of a bank or finance house – except that Hayes took the real risks. The others didn't loan money until you more or less proved you didn't need it. 'These people you turn down – ever hear what happens to them?'

'Sometimes.' Suddenly, Hayes screwed his flabby face into a grin and wagged a forefinger. 'Now I've got it – you're on no "tidying up". What you're really asking is, Do I know if any of them got involved with The Tallyman. Right?'

'Maybe.' Thane leaned one hand on the desk. 'Well, *did* they?'

Slowly, the man shook his head. 'They might – I wouldn't know. If they did, I'm sorry for them.'

'You can still help,' said Thane, leaning forward. 'I want the names of people you've turned down lately.'

'No.' Hayes snapped the word. 'I guarantee secrecy to anyone who comes up that stair. Break that, and I'm half-way out of business.'

'I could get a warrant to go through your files –'

'It wouldn't do any good.' Hayes tapped his forehead. 'My reject file is up here, nowhere else. Look, Chief Inspector, I'll give you the real reason. I just don't want to get involved – involved with you or The Tallyman.'

'Scared?'

'That's it. Scared stiff. I talked about Fergan because he said he'd been here and it was a murder case. But this is different.' The money-lender rubbed a hand tenderly along his jawline. 'I feel bad enough as it is. But – well, tooth-ache's not permanent.'

Thane's mouth tightened. But he sensed it would take a lot of pressure to budge Hayes – pressure and time. 'I'll leave it – for now. But I'll be back.'

'Just make it after working hours,' grunted the money-lender. He got up, went through the hall again with Thane, and undid the doorlocks.

'Rab' – Thane made a last try as the door swung open – 'tallymen are scum.'

'Or worse,' agreed Hayes wearily. He sighed. 'Look, if it helps keep you off my back, there's one thing I've heard. The Tallyman doesn't always need repayments in cash.'

'Meaning?'

'I wouldn't know. You just – well, hear things.'

The door closed. On the other side the locks began to clatter into place.

When Thane got back down to the car the snow was really falling. He had to use a glove to brush the worst of it from the windows before he climbed aboard and restarted the engine.

One down, one to go. Whatever Rab Hayes might know, he was too scared to talk. Well, at least the second man on his list didn't scare easily.

Though even that might be a drawback.

As far as Harry Freeman was concerned, Monday night was club night. The rest of the week he ran one of the biggest bookmaking businesses in Glasgow and ran it squarely.

But Monday night was a ritual. The only time anyone could remember Harry being absent from the Lombok Club was when the Six Days' War blew up. Then the tall, dark-haired bookmaker was absent for a couple of weeks – to return with a limp, a grin, a string bag crammed with Jaffa oranges and a new ashtray which had once been a Russian tank-shell cartridge.

The Lombok was in Central Division territory, not far from Sauchiehall Street. Colin Thane showed his warrant card at the door, left his coat, gave a reassuring nod to the hovering manager, and walked up to the first floor.

The roulette tables were busy, the main sound a low monotony of clicking wheels. Glasgow took gambling like it did most pleasures – seriously.

Thane lit a cigarette, glanced around, and saw his man. Dressed like a lawyer, Harry Freeman was hovering on the fringe of the Number One table with a pensive expression on his face. Thane crossed over.

'Winning, Harry?'

Freeman turned and grinned. 'Losing. So far I've saved myself four hundred quid.'

It was a joke most people knew about. Harry Freeman, bookmaker, didn't gamble . . . except in terms of the imaginary bets he placed on each spin of the wheel and the imaginary profit-and-loss account he kept in his head. But he loved every minute of the mental exercise.

On the table the wheel slowed. The ball took a last, hesitant quiver, then settled on zero. There was a universal groan.

'Buy you a drink,' offered the bookmaker.

'With *your* losses?' Thane jingled the change in his pocket. 'My turn.'

'This happens to be a private club, Chief Inspector,' reminded Freeman, still grinning. 'You want the place raided or something?'

They went over to the bar, ordered two single-malt whiskies, added a modicum of water, and sipped for a moment.

'Well, Colin?' Freeman raised an expectant eyebrow. 'What's happening?'

Thane shrugged. He'd known Harry Freeman since schooldays. At least once they'd tried to punch each other's heads off. 'I'm going after The Tallyman.'

'Oh.' The bookmaker's eyes narrowed a fraction. 'Because of the Fergan business?' He nursed his glass, starting the liquor swirling. 'I told you all that happened with me, remember? Fergan placed a few bets, then I stopped his credit. I've written off what he owed – it wasn't too much. He hit some bookies a lot worse.'

'You tried to collect.'

It was Freeman's turn to shrug. 'A few reminders, then on the black list. You know how it is in Scotland – a client can sue a bookie if he doesn't pay up. But not the other way round. And I'm a businessman, not a back-street heavy.'

'That's why I'm here.'

'Compliment taken.' Freeman leaned back against the bar. 'The place is busy tonight.'

Thane followed the gaze. Most of the people around the tables were 'fun' players. They'd bought a handful of chips and, win or lose, that was their lot. But here and there you could spot the serious ones . . . the middle-aged women with notebook, pencil and a system, the small scowling men who'd do without sleep if necessary.

And then there were others. Nervous ones. The man at Number Two table sucking his teeth as if he'd never stop. Or at Number Four, the youngster in his early twenties, quietly dressed, with short fair hair. He was leaning forward, pale face intent, fists clenched at his side, every muscle tensed. He lost, edged back a little, and began counting the remaining chips in his hands.

'That's life, laddie,' murmured Freeman to himself. 'You'll learn.'

'Know him?' asked Thane.

'Just the face. He's been in before.' The bookmaker's voice remained little more than a whisper. 'But try the baccarat game, gently. Bow tie and small cigar.'

Thane finished his drink, turned casually to lay the glass on the bar, and had his chance as he swung round again.

The man was to the left of the table, spectating, the cheroot little more than a stub between his lips. He wore a green-check suit, his face was thin with a small scar under the left eye, and he'd mousy, thinning hair. His name was Herb Cullen. He'd once served a five-stretch for armed robbery.

'You've some nice members,' mused Thane.

'Him?' Freeman grimaced. 'He'll have a one-night ticket in his pocket.' The bookmaker's manner changed. 'Later, Colin – we've company.'

The couple approaching were hand-in-hand. The man, slim, wearing rimless spectacles, was in his early thirties. He was thin-faced, with long, copper-coloured hair. The girl, slightly younger, was good-looking in a raw-boned, high-breasted way. Raven hair piled high, she wore a mid-length kaftan dress in deep blue with yellow silk braiding.

37

Both had the kind of tan which came expensive in the Scottish winter.

'Harry, nice to see you,' greeted the man. Behind the spectacles his eyes were a rather watery blue. The voice was a cool, hard-to-place drawl. 'How's the horse business?'

'The favourites keep winning.' Freeman smiled at the girl. 'Hello, Helen, still keeping bad company?'

'Till something better comes along.' She returned the smile with interest. 'I haven't met your friend.'

The bookmaker made an apologetic noise. 'Well, let's say more or less a friend. Chief Inspector Thane, this is Helen – Helen Milne. And Josh Barbar.'

They exchanged the usual greetings, then Barbar eyed Thane with curious interest. 'You're Millside Division, aren't you? That means you're off base a little.'

'Even Chief Inspectors let people buy them drinks,' said Freeman easily. 'Still, better be friendly to him, Colin. He might offer you a job in your dotage.'

'Barbar – the collection agency?' Thane nodded his understanding. 'What about you, then, Mr Barbar? Here purely on pleasure?'

'Fifty-fifty.' Barbar thumbed towards the bar. 'I've started a new operation, a bonded security service. The Lombok Club are customers.' There was a small wooden plaque above the bar mirror. In gold letters circling a lion's head were the words 'Protected by Barbar Security.'

'Protected? You mean you've some men around?' Thane's professional curiosity was aroused.

Barbar shook his head. His long hair fell loose across his spectacles and he brushed it back. 'No, we simply do cash runs to and from the bank for them. It's early days, but we've signed some other contracts – supplying store detectives, that kind of thing.'

'Not what you'd call competition, Chief Inspector,' said the girl cheerfully. 'Not yet, anyway – though you'd imagine he was ready to make a take-over bid for the city force, the way he talks about it.'

'It's a living.' Barbar glanced at her. 'Let's get that drink, Helen. Ah – how about you two?'

They shook their heads. The girl smiled again and the couple moved off.

'Remind me not to run up any unpaid bills,' said Thane wryly. 'Who's the girl?'

'Helen?' Freeman pursed his lips. 'Her father's a doctor – heart specialist and a good one. I've known him for a spell. Plenty of money in the background. Barbar's different. He hauled himself up from somewhere a few years back, started a collection agency over in the East End, and – well, there's no shortage of business. Now he's in the city, the cheaper end, runs a fast car and has a pretty expensive flat in the West End.'

Thane nodded and lit another cigarette. 'We were talking about someone else, Harry.'

'I know.' Harry Freeman rubbed his chin and looked longingly towards the roulette tables. 'Well, about all I've heard is that The Tallyman's no myth. And he can play pretty rough.'

'Nothing else?'

'Not much.' The bookmaker eyed him quizzically. 'There's something you want. Let's have it.'

'Fergan landed in debt because he played the horses.'

'I'm no welfare organization, Colin.' Freeman frowned at his feet. 'A mug is a mug. Anyone who bets more than he can afford to lose is asking for it.'

'And you pay taxes,' concluded Thane dryly. 'I want some names – people on the black list, punters who've run out of credit in a big way. And you don't come into anything, now or later.'

'I've heard that before.' Harry Freeman whistled lightly between his teeth for a moment, then nodded. 'Anything else?'

'That depends on *you*.'

'You were always damned good at twisting arms.' The bookmaker looked beyond him and his manner suddenly changed. 'Time you were going.'

'Why?'

'Bow tie and small cigar – Herb Cullen. He just left. Somebody somewhere told me Cullen did time with the late Mr Laverick – and knew him pretty well.'

'Well enough to be his minder?'

'All I do is run a book.' Freeman winked, grinned, and limped towards the clicking wheels.

Thane lost a full, impatient minute downstairs, waiting while a harassed cloakroom girl located his coat. When he did get outside, the street seemed empty and the snow, still feathering down, had cut the street lamps' visibility.

Cursing, Thane looked around and gave up. But as he started to walk towards the car he heard a loud clatter and a muffled cry of pain. The cry sounded again, from the mouth of an alleyway.

He ran, the steps muffled in the white blanket underfoot. The alley was a dark tunnel of night, but as he entered a man came from a black patch of doorway. He went over, almost tripped on a garbage bin which had been thrown on its side and saw a vague shape just beyond.

Thane found his cigarette lighter, sparked it, and the tiny flame showed a pale young face, a blood-smeared mouth and tousled fair hair. The youngster from the roulette table was trying to haul himself back up on his feet.

A car door slammed further along. He extinguished the lighter and swung round. Red taillights glowed, a starter-motor growled. He took a few steps, then stopped as the engine fired and the car roared off. At the far end of the alley it swung left on to the roadway, still gathering speed.

A corner of his mind registered it was a cream late-model Ford Cortina. There hadn't been a chance to get the licence plate.

He went back, reached the doorway, and stared. The youngster was gone. There was no sign of him in the street, and the snow was thickening.

Feeling like a rookie constable who'd made a mess of things, he slogged again to the doorway and used the lighter. There was a small patch of blood on the snow. Already it was beginning to disappear.

Shivering, swearing, he decided to call it a night.

Chapter Three

Inevitably, Phil Moss had arrived by the time he got home. The scent of herbal cigarettes hung in the air like low-grade incense, and Moss was hunkered down on the living-room floor with Tommy, investigating the interior of a broken-down friction-drive space capsule.

Neither bothered to look up as Thane entered. Even the dog, sprawled in front of the electric radiator, contented itself with a brief yawn in Thane's direction.

'Don't let me disturb anyone,' said Thane caustically. He looked around. 'Where's Mary – and Kate?'

'In the kitchen, getting supper.' Moss attempted a spot of fine adjustment with a penknife. The knife slipped and he swore. 'Man, they build these things like booby-traps!'

'Looks like it.' Thane dropped into a chair. 'How'd the Cub session go, Tommy?'

'Just the usual.' The nine-year-old took the knife while Moss still sucked blood, gave a couple of swift twists, and had the job complete. 'That's it now, Uncle Phil.'

'Eh . . . yes.' Moss hauled himself to his feet, wrapping a frayed, off-white handkerchief around the gash. 'That's what I was going to do.'

Thane chuckled and drew a glare. But Moss left it at that as the door opened and Mary came in with a tray of coffee and sandwiches.

'Still snowing outside, Colin?' she asked mildly.

He nodded.

'I thought so – you left a trail of the stuff through the hall.' She glanced at Tommy and thumbed towards the door. 'You – bed. Now. It's late.'

'But Kate –'

'Is on her way. There's a glass of milk for you in the kitchen.'

An expression on his face one stage short of rebellion, the boy headed for the door. Then he stopped, looked back, and grinned. 'Do you know what Uncle Phil said when he cut himself, Mum?'

'I can guess.' Mary pointed again. 'Bed.'

She laid down the tray as he went off, grumbling.

'Just two cups?' queried Thane.

'I'll have mine in the kitchen.' She looked at him pointedly. 'I thought you might like to talk to Phil – about things.'

'Things? What things?' Moss switched his attention to the sandwiches. 'Mind me asking what's in these, Mary?'

'I'd be surprised if you didn't,' she said dryly, then weakened. 'Stick to the ones on the left, Phil. They're plain egg. Colin's got his usual – what's in them would sink a battleship.'

'Then stay and watch,' suggested Thane.

'I've ironing to do.' She said it in a way which didn't leave room for argument. 'You'll want to talk.'

Once she'd gone, Moss helped himself to coffee, made another cautious check of the sandwiches, then began eating.

'What are we supposed to talk about?' he queried.

'Just things in general.' Thane joined him and gathered his own supply. 'Did you get those photographs?'

'Uh-huh.' Moss pointed his cup towards a large envelope propped against the TV set. 'And MacLeod got back from the Turkish Raven just before I left. We've a few

43

names of regulars who've either signed the pledge or moved to another bar. How'd *you* make out?'

'I saw some people. One of them was Herb Cullen. Remember him?'

Moss frowned, his jaws working busily. 'Wears a scar, sometimes carries a gun – uh-huh.'

'And probably drives a cream Ford Cortina.' Thane gave him a capsuled rundown on the evening, from his visit to Rab Hayes onward.

'The youngster in the lane sounds like trouble,' mused Moss. 'And if Cullen is a minder –'

'Then we're luckier than we deserve.' Thane crossed to collect the photographic envelope.

The *Evening Bugle* cameraman hadn't skimped on his task. There were over sixty pictures in the envelope, all glossy ten-by-eight enlargements – people arriving at the High Court, people departing, people standing around in groups or all alone. Thane found one of himself. Most of the results were pin-sharp, though occasionally only the back of a head had been captured.

'I've been through them already,' said Moss. He shook his head at Thane's silent query. 'Let's wait and see what you come across.'

They started, taking the prints one by one, building up a reject heap, setting a few aside as they spotted a familiar face. The last of the coffee grew cold.

Near the bottom of the pile, Thane suddenly stopped, frowned, and pointed.

'Who's that – in the background, Phil, getting out of the taxi?'

'With the girl?' Moss belched, but softly – a concession to where he was – and grinned a little. 'Trucks Harris, and that's his brand new wife . . . heaven help her.' He flicked a fingernail at the ned's face. 'I checked. He's a defence witness in a Southern Division stabbing.'

'Doing his duty as a citizen?' Thane's voice was acid.

Harris had been in the dock on a murder charge only six months before, but the Southern case hadn't quite made it.

The first run-through finished, they went back to the selection they'd set aside. In six photographs they had a total of eight men with Criminal Records files. Moss could discount five of the faces – either they'd business at court or a friend was making an appearance. Neds often turned up in that way, drawn by a mixture of idle curiosity and a liking to be seen around where it mattered.

That left three. Thane discarded another, an elderly safe-blower who was more or less retired and found time on his hands.

'These two, Phil. We'll check them out tomorrow – but no direct contact.'

Moss nodded. Titch Alexander and Sandy Lang were both possibles. Alexander was small, fat, and greasy. He'd half-a-dozen convictions for violence. Sandy Lang – a face in a group, occupying less than half an inch of glossy surface but unmistakable with buck teeth, receding chin and a small, patchy beard – usually worked as a con man but hadn't been noticeably active for some time.

'I'll fix it. What about tonight's little business with Herb Cullen? Do we collect him?'

'Yes, but let's have a reason – something pretty solid, yet far away from The Tallyman business. And we'll have to start some cross-checking the moment Harry Freeman comes through with his list. We might be lucky.'

Moss made a noncommittal noise, found his herbal cigarettes, lit one, and spluttered over the first draw. He gulped for breath and recovered. 'Look, what about the Barbar Agency? Couldn't we have a word with them? They're professionals in the bad-debt business. I know a retired Central man who worked with them for a spell. He said they stuck to the rules –'

Thane shook his head. 'Barbar seems a shrewd enough operator. But leave them out of it.'

'Why?'

'Because there's the other side, Phil. The Barbar Agency deals in people in debt, people who need money badly. It could be exactly the kind of organization where The Tallyman has a contact, someone feeding him names and addresses from the files. I don't want to scare anyone – not yet.'

'Then that's it?' Moss yawned, scratched his scrawny stomach, and fastened his jacket.

'Uh-huh. Except' – Thane hesitated – 'Phil, I'll need to take an hour or so off tomorrow morning. Personal business, around ten a.m.'

'Something wrong?'

Feeling sheepish, Thane shook his head. 'I – uh – just have to see someone.'

'In town?' Moss's curiosity was roused.

'In town,' agreed Thane. 'All right?'

A slightly querulous flicker crossed the thin face opposite. Then Moss shrugged. 'Right. What's the story if Buddha starts screaming for you?'

'Tell him I'm – I'm at the bank.'

He steered Moss to the door, said goodnight, and watched him head off through the snow towards the bus stop at the end of the road. Then he closed the door and went through to the kitchen. Mary had finished her ironing.

'What did Phil think?' she demanded.

'About what?'

She gave an exasperated sigh. 'About the bank job – you told him, didn't you?'

'No. I thought I'd wait till I'd had the interview,' he said awkwardly.

'But – ' She stopped and shook her head. 'Never mind.

46

Let's get to bed early for once, before that damned phone starts ringing.'

'Tonight?' Thane gave a lopsided grin. 'Things should be quiet. It's too cold for trouble.'

He woke before the alarm next morning, took an unusual amount of care over shaving, and found Mary had laid out his best suit and the new shirt. By the time he'd dressed and headed downstairs, breakfast was ready. Outside, the snow had stopped falling but was lying thick.

'Stand still.' Mary inspected him carefully. 'No, not that tie. The knitted blue one goes better.'

Obediently, he went back and switched ties, then returned to the kitchen. Inevitably, he dripped coffee on the suit and it had to be sponged off. Eating, he couldn't remember when he'd felt less hungry.

'Time I woke the kids,' said Mary, glancing at the wall clock.

'And I'll need to go.' He pushed his chair back.

'But it's early –'

'I don't want to get caught up in a last-minute rush.' He kissed her. 'Shouldn't you wish me luck or something?'

'You know I do.' She hesitated. 'Colin, at the bank – you won't decide right away? Straight off, I mean?'

'We'll talk about it first,' he promised.

It was still dark outside and the car took a couple of minutes starting with full choke and a weak battery. The roads were slippery until he reached where the gritting trucks had been operating.

It was a little before eight a.m. when Thane reached Millside and left the Austin in the station yard. He went into the building through the rear entrance, past the radio room and the telephone switchboard, nodded to MacArthur, the duty uniformed branch inspector, and went upstairs.

The main C.I.D. room had the usual predawn smell of used air and stale cigarette smoke. The d.c.s were gossiping quietly in a corner. When they saw him they separated quickly, muttering good morning. And there was a light burning in the little cubbyhole of an office which Phil Moss occupied.

Thane sensed trouble. He rapped once on the glass of his second-in-command's door and went in.

'I thought you'd be early.' Moss was at his desk, sleepy-eyed, unshaven, looking more rumpled than ever. 'We've had a – well, a wee bit of bad luck.'

'Where?'

'The Alhambra warehouse.' Despite himself, Moss yawned. 'We ended the watch on it last night, remember? So it was done about two o'clock this morning. The beat man discovered it.'

Thane felt a dull, chill anger. 'How bad?'

'Bad enough. They cleaned out that load of transistor radios and twenty colour television sets. The TV sets were only delivered yesterday – maybe they were waiting on them.'

'Why didn't you let me know?'

Moss shrugged 'The night shift phoned me first, and you've this "personal business" thing on. I thought you could probably use the sleep.' If Moss had noticed the best suit and the rest, he didn't comment.

'Who's working on it now?'

'Mathieson and Contine mainly – they've got a night watchman from nearby who noticed a truck driving away, but not much more. I'd reckon it was a three-man operation – a driver lookout and two doing the loading. They got in at the rear, then forced the main door from inside. We dug out the warehouse manager, and he reckons there's about nine thousand quid's worth gone.'

'At least it's under the line.' Thane knew a slightly guilty relief. You wouldn't find it in a rulebook, but any case with a loss into five figures was automatically hoisted into the 'major crime' bracket as far as Headquarters was concerned. That meant reports every time anyone sneezed, Regional Crime men wandering in for pep-talk sessions, the prospect of an unhappy little entry in the Chief Constable's annual report. 'What about you, Phil – feel like taking a break now?'

'Breakfast and a shave will do.' Moss eased himself upright. 'We could have done without this business, that's for sure. The Tallyman's enough for anyone's plate.'

'It's happened – and we might as well get some benefit from it.' Thane opened the door, looked out, and beckoned the nearest of the hovering d.c.s. 'Beech –'

Detective Constable Beech, a young man with an unhappy habit of falling foul of authority, came forward cautiously.

'Sir?'

'The Alhambra job – I want you to pick up a middle-weight ned called Herb Cullen. It's a "help us with inquiries" approach, but bring him in. Get his details from Records, and ask uniformed branch to lay on a car and a couple of men.'

'Right, sir.' Beech, relieved that the little matter of his previous week's expense account hadn't been mentioned, turned to go.

'Beech' – Thane stopped him – 'if there's the slightest hint of trouble you'll secure the prisoner.'

'On inquiries only, sir?' Beech raised an eyebrow. Handcuffs usually came later, much later – when they were needed at all.

'Cullen doesn't like cops.'

'That's surprising,' said Beech solemnly.

Thane kept back the grin till Beech was gone.

'It might be worthwhile turning over Cullen's place,' mused Moss. 'But we'd need a warrant –'

'We'll get one,' said Thane calmly. 'You'll do the rest while he's here.'

'I'd a feeling that was coming.' Moss rasped a thumbnail

across his patchy stubble. 'All right, but you're sticking your neck out.'

'I didn't notice. Done anything about our two possibles from the court photographs?'

'Headquarters said they'd check.'

'Fine.' Thane thumbed towards the door. 'On your way, then. I've work to do.'

There was plenty waiting when he went through to his room – overnight reports, the list of Millside prisoners due to make lower-court appearances on remand, the inevitable circulars from Headquarters. Thane buzzed the duty orderly, had him bring a mug of tea, and sorted out the pile of paperwork.

An envelope addressed to him and marked 'By Hand' was lying near the bottom. Curious, he opened it, then gave a soft murmur of surprise. It was from Harry Freeman, scrawled in a spidery longhand.

'When you want things you're usually in a hurry. Hope this helps,' said the brief note which was the first page. 'I've another idea, but I'll let you know about it later.'

He flicked over. The bookmaker had attached a list of almost a dozen names and addresses, the amount each defaulting punter owed arranged alongside. Freeman must have sat up late to complete it.

For another full minute he looked at the list, the names meaning nothing in themselves yet providing a focusing point. Then, at last, he flipped the desk intercom switch.

'Sir?' The duty orderly answered through what sounded like a mouthful of bacon roll.

'Sergeant MacLeod arrived yet?'

He heard a hasty swallowing noise and the orderly's voice became clearer. 'He's here now, sir.'

'Ask him to come through.' Thane released the switch, then swore to himself as the telephone rang. He lifted the receiver, jammed it between ear and shoulder, and reached for a cigarette.

'Thane –'

'Records Office here, Chief Inspector,' crackled a girl's voice in his ear. Headquarters were turning more and more desk work over to the women police constables and civilian staff on the principle that any fit and healthy cop was better employed out thief-catching. 'You asked for information on two men, Alexander and Lang.'

'That's right,' he agreed. 'And why they'd want to look in at yesterday's High Court.'

The door had opened, Sergeant MacLeod, a large, slow-moving individual, poked his head round and Thane waved him in.

'We can help a little.' The girl sounded small and blonde, which meant she was probably the opposite. 'Alexander is on file as a former associate of James Simond, who has previous convictions. Simond was sentenced to three years for serious assault yesterday – his case was in the south courtroom. We've a fairly strong hint that Alexander will be – well, looking after Mrs Simond.'

Thane chuckled.

Records had built up their 'gossip' section fairly recently. It dealt in trivia, apparently meaningless items fed in by anyone from contacts and beat men upwards. It meant a lot of work, of indexing and cross-checking. But sometimes a string of apparently unrelated items would click together, point to a new suspicious partnership or a job being planned.

'What about Lang?' he asked.

'Nothing to involve him with yesterday's court.' She sounded almost apologetic. 'But we've got a note that he's located in an apartment block in Central Division. At least he was a few days ago.'

He noted the address, thanked her, and hung up. Then he turned to the waiting MacLeod. 'Mac, I wanted to see you about those names you collected last night.'

51

'At the Turkish Raven – aye.' The sergeant carefully cleared his throat. 'You'll need them checked out now?'

'All of them, plus these.' Thane slid Harry Freeman's list across the desk. 'You know what we're after?'

'Inspector Moss briefed me last night.' MacLeod's brow furrowed. 'They're not likely to be cooperative, sir.'

'And they've every right to tell us to go to hell,' agreed Thane. 'Plain domestic troubles are normally none of our business. But use your native Highland charm, Mac.' He grinned at the man encouragingly. 'Why not start at their homes – try their wives, or whatever they've got?'

'Wives.' MacLeod looked unhappier than ever. 'Can I take a w.p.c. along with me?'

Thane sighed. 'Mac, you're fat, damned near fifty and going bald. You look as respectable as a church elder –'

'And Marine Division picked up a church elder on an indecency charge last week,' reminded MacLeod gloomily. 'Ach, I just don't trust women on their own. Say the wrong word and they're liable to start screaming from the nearest window.'

He capitulated with a sigh and a final warning. 'We have to take it easy with those people, Mac. All we can do is ask them to help.'

Once MacLeod had gone, Thane glanced at his watch, then took a long draw on his cigarette. One more hour and he'd be at the bank, starting that interview. He frowned uneasily. Any other day and he'd have taken a trip out to the Alhambra warehouse business. Or would have been probing a little around outfits like the Barbar Agency. No matter how many ex-cops Josh Barbar had on his payroll.

There was knock on the door and Phil Moss strolled in. The Millside second-in-command had shaved, was using a toothpick on the last of his breakfast, and seemed much happier.

'I've got the Cullen search warrant organized,' he announced. 'I'll collect it on the way.'

'Good. ' Thane stubbed his cigarette. 'Sandy Lang's our possible from those pictures, Phil. I don't think he's the type who'd show his nose inside a court without some kind of reason.'

'Like reporting back to someone.' Moss nodded, an idea of his own to put forward. 'How about the Lombok Club? We could do a little quiet asking about Cullen and that youngster.'

'Then someone tells someone we asked –' Thane shook his head firmly. 'Not yet, Phil.'

The intercom buzzed. He turned and pressed the switch.

'Yes?'

'Detective Constable Beech with a Mr Cullen,' said the duty orderly impassively.

'Send them straight in.' He closed the switch, looked at Moss, and winked.

Phil Moss opened the door, then squeezed out at the same time as Beech eased Herb Cullen into the room.

'Mr Cullen,' said Beech briefly, keeping a deceptively light finger-and-thumb grip on the man's left cuff.

'Nice of him to come.' Thane noted that Cullen's mousy hair was tousled and he wasn't wearing a tie. But the thin, scarred face between was a frozen mask. 'Any trouble?'

Beech shook his head. 'None worth mentioning, sir. He was still in bed when we arrived.'

'Out late last night, Cullen?' queried Thane mildly.

'Maybe.' Cullen shrugged with what was meant to be philosophical ease. 'What's it this time?'

'We're interested in where you were last night.'

He saw what might have been a flicker of caution. But Cullen was no stranger to this kind of routine. He twisted a sardonic grin. 'Same place as you – the Lombok Club.

53

But I won't be back, mister – I don't like the kind o' people they let in.'

Slowly, Thane got to his feet and came round to the front of the desk. 'Never mind the comedy. What about afterwards? Round about two o'clock this morning, for instance?'

'Why?' The man asked it easily, with a new confidence. 'What happened then?'

'I asked where you were,' reminded Thane stonily.

'With some people – at a friend's place.'

'And nowhere near the Alhambra warehouse in King Street?'

Cullen grinned openly. 'Never heard of it.'

'No? Yet we've a witness who –' Thane stopped and made a convincing business of scowling. 'All right, what's your friend's name?'

'Well, he's a – a kind of a friend of a friend,' hedged Cullen, cautious again. 'Look, Chief Inspector, I wasn't near any warehouse – that's the full strength. Give me an hour an' I'll bring in half a dozen people who'll tell you the same.'

'Or two hours and you'll make it a dozen?' Thane grunted, glanced at Beech, then turned back to the waiting, scar-faced thug. 'Turn out your pockets.'

Silently, Cullen obeyed. As the collection grew, Thane prodded a gold cigarette lighter. 'Expensive.'

'Bought an' paid for,' snapped Cullen.

'Of course.' He picked up the man's wallet and unhurriedly checked it through. 'Close on fifty pounds. Petty cash?'

'I might need bus fares.'

'Most of us do,' agreed Thane wryly. 'Looks like you're earning good money. A steady job?'

The uneasiness came back. 'No. Just – just casual deals. An' a bit luck last night at the Lombok.'

'I see.' Thane nodded to the expressionless, waiting Beech. 'Hold him for now.'

'Wait a minute,' protested Cullen. 'What charge?'

'No charge – yet.' Thane stopped as the telephone shrilled. He lifted the receiver and heard Buddha Ilford's voice. 'Hold on a second, sir –' He covered the mouthpiece and grinned at Cullen. 'You're just a good citizen helping us with inquiries.' Gesturing towards the desk, he added, 'You'll get a receipt for this stuff.'

'I'd better. And the money's counted, friend.' Cullen spun on his heel and headed out, Beech having to move fast to catch up.

The door closed and Thane removed his hand from the phone. 'Sorry, sir – I'm ready now.'

'Busy morning?' Chief Superintendent Ilford seemed in surprisingly good humour.

'Shaping that way,' agreed Thane. 'And the Alhambra warehouse job didn't help.'

Ilford's laugh rasped along the line. 'You'll survive. The warehouse thing is one reason for calling. You'll get a teletype in a minute from Eastern Division. They've found the truck that was used – at least it looks that way. Stolen last night, abandoned sometime this morning. A nylon-stocking mask left on the front seat and bits of a broken crate in the rear. The truck's being fingerprinted. Anything fresh from your end?'

'Still working on it, sir.'

'Divisional stock answer number one,' rumbled the C.I.D. chief. 'All right, what about The Tallyman?'

'Better. I may have a lead to the ned who was Laverick's minder – and we've another possible.' Thane remembered his Division manpower, quickly becoming stretched. 'It would help if Central Division could put a long-distance tail on one of their locals.'

'Name?'

He gave Ilford the details.

'I'll fix it,' promised Ilford. 'Ah . . . I've a little piece of news from the Chief Constable. You can pass it around.'

'Sir?'

'Last quarter's crime returns are down almost two per cent. He's very happy.' The voice became different. 'That warehouse job won't help this quarter, unless we tidy it.'

'Yes, sir.'

Ilford grunted and hung up.

Grimacing, Thane replaced his own receiver. The detective constables in the main office would be more interested in some news about that three-per-cent wage increase the Police Federation was howling for. But the statistics still mattered – the city was running at a level of around 44,000 crimes and 60,000 offences a year.

They were arresting and convicting in about one case in three. If that didn't sound impressive it was still better than national average, damned near miraculous in a force four hundred under its authorized strength of three thousand and sixty. Men were leaving faster than new recruits joined – and the physical and educational standards set were tough, maybe too tough. Out of around a thousand would-be applicants a year, preliminary thinning and changes of mind meant only about two hundred being called for interview and examination. Perhaps two thirds of those two hundred finally drew uniforms as rookie cops, and even then several bailed out quickly once they'd sampled the life.

Thane didn't blame them. He remembered the overtime sheet he'd seen a couple of weeks back at Headquarters. In one week the city C.I.D. had, on its own, piled up seventeen hundred hours overtime. That was just about average as things were. Overtime working had been creeping upward for more years than he cared to remember.

He caught himself thinking about the bank again. He swore, went out into the main office, and spent the next few minutes making life grim and earnest for the few d.c.s working at the desks.

When he'd finished, he felt much better.

Cold and shivering, a drip on the end of his nose, Detective Inspector Moss made a complaining reappearance minutes before ten a.m. He stopped at the sight of Thane standing in coat and hat, ready to leave, and raised an eyebrow.

'Something up?'

'That personal thing I've to do.' Thane cleared his throat with a niggling sense of guilt. 'Phil, I've left a note on your desk. It'll bring you up to date. What about Cullen's house?'

'Room and kitchen two up in Claver Street. But he's spent plenty of money inside. It's got –'

'Find anything?'

'Uh-huh.' Moss took an agonizing time to locate his notebook, then didn't bother to open it. 'Four hundred pounds cash hidden in a shoe, a Beretta automatic under a loose floorboard – I put it back after I did a wee thing to the firing pin – and a couple of telephone numbers. They were on the back of an old envelope I found in the waste bucket.'

'You've left things as they were?'

'Mostly. There's just enough of a difference to make it look as though we went over the place for something fairly big.'

'And the telephone numbers – checked them?'

'Give me a chance.' Indignant, Moss wiped a sleeve across his nose. 'Colin, there's no phone in Cullen's place. And the last time a public phone worked around Claver Street the Post Office practically declared a national holiday. People don't just wreck public phones there – they pinch the doors off the kiosks while they're at it.'

'Right. Keep quiet about the gun and find out about

those numbers.' Thane started on his way. 'I'll be about an hour . . .'

'Where?'

It was too late. Moss watched the tall, broad-shouldered figure stride towards the stairway and frowned, ignoring his ulcer's low-key mid-morning twinge. Well, maybe it was none of his business. Except that he knew Colin Thane. And if he was right, then that same tall figure was hustling towards a big mistake.

Founded 1821, total funds £37,000,000, the Bank of Central Scotland's head office was a squat granite block in Harald Street, close to the heart of Glasgow's business centre. The four-storey building was currently swathed in a lacework of snow-crusted tubular scaffolding, the stonework being cleaned to remove a decade's soot and bird droppings.

A clock mounted above the main door registered five minutes past the hour as Thane swung his car into a parking space. He jammed a coin into the waiting meter, hurried along, propelled his way through the bank's revolving door at a rate which alarmed a fat woman on her way out, and headed for the inquiry counter.

'Sir?' The counter clerk, sleek and well-combed, stepped forward.

'I've an appointment – with Mr Daill, the general manager.'

'And the name, sir?' The clerk's polite deference switched to maximum.

'Thane.'

He looked around while the clerk used a house phone. The bank's interior was a mixture of terrazzo floors, mahogany panelling and marble pillars. Long counters had a number of customers scattered along their length. But there was an almost overpowering atmosphere of cathedral-like calm. This was a high temple of business,

58

where the noise level seemed restricted to the rustle of paper money.

A messenger went by, neat in a red frock coat and carrying an anonymous brown-paper parcel. He went through a small door, giving a brief glimpse of cups on a desk and someone in shirt-sleeves. The sight was vaguely reassuring.

'Mr Thane . . .' the clerk had replaced the house phone. 'If you'll go across to the far end and take the elevator to the top floor – you're expected.'

He found the elevator waiting. It was a self-operating unit and Thane pressed the fourth-floor button. As the cage began rising he checked his tie, then spotted a splash of mud on one shoe. He rubbed it off on the opposite trouser cuff.

The elevator stopped and he stepped out into a carpeted corridor.

A woman secretary, middle-aged and neat as they came, greeted him with a smile and guided him along to a door marked 'Private.' She knocked, opened it, and ushered him in.

It was a large room, with a hand-woven Chinese carpet and a broad expanse of window looking out across the city. A heavily built, florid-faced man looked up from behind a king-sized desk which had a tiny intercom box on one side and two telephones on the other.

'Chief Inspector Thane?' The man rose to his feet. 'I'm Daill – Patterson Daill.'

The Central Scotland's general manager was all the things a successful banker should be – slightly paunchy, well-groomed, with gold-rimmed old-fashioned spectacles and a clerical-grey suit giving just a glimpse of watch chain. Daill was fond of boasting he'd come all the way up from office-boy – which was true, though a favourite uncle had been on the board of directors.

They shook hands, and Daill gestured towards a chair.

'I'm late,' apologized Thane. 'I'm sorry.'

'These things happen.' Daill made a sympathetic noise and settled again behind the desk. There wasn't a scrap of paper on its surface. 'Well, I'm delighted you could come.' He built a steeple with his fingertips. 'Were you surprised by our letter?'

'That's an understatement.' Thane grinned a little. 'I don't even have a bank account with you.'

'Quite.' The banker made it clear he considered that an error of judgement. He produced a cigarette case, flicked it open, and offered it. Thane took one and accepted a light. Daill replaced the case. 'Now, Chief Inspector, you know little about us, but we know quite sufficient about you.' He smiled slightly. 'It is normal banking practice to make – ah – discreet inquiries before coming to decisions.'

Nodding, Thane looked around for the ashtray.

'Appointing an executive security officer is a new departure for this bank,' mused Daill. 'The board gave it particularly careful consideration and decided it was a vital part of any modern image. Then when it came to deciding who we should approach there was the inevitable list of possible candidates –'

Thane cut him short. 'Mr Daill.'

'Yes?' The man blinked.

'I didn't come here to play party games.' Thane tried to keep his anger under control. 'The old cigarette-but-no-ashtray trick is one of the oldest in the book. And if you've any more management-selection-type gimmicks lined up, let's call it a day.'

Wordlessly, Daill opened a drawer and slid an ashtray across the desk. He produced the cigarette case again and lit one of his own.

'No more, Chief Inspector,' he promised wryly. 'I – ah – I'm sorry. It wasn't my idea. Now, what was I saying?'

'That you've a list of possible runners for the job.'

'No, that we had *one*,' corrected the banker hastily. 'And

it was decided to approach you first. Does the post seem attractive?'

'Interesting. But what's involved?'

'You'd be our security consultant.' Daill unbent a little. 'We've roughly a hundred branches, town and country. Some could be robbed by a five-year-old. We want that changed. But of course you'd be based here, at head office . . . with senior executive status. And – ah – naturally, we'd provide a car.' He spread his hands wide. 'Does that answer?'

'It's a good offer,' agreed Thane slowly.

'And the salary?'

'Good too.'

'Then the decision is yours, Chief Inspector.' The banker seemed relieved. 'Now, why not have a quick glimpse of the place. Then you'll want a little time to consider your answer. This is Tuesday. Our board meet again on Friday. Supposing we say you answer two days from now – Thursday at ten a.m.?'

He'd have liked longer, but he nodded.

'Excellent.' Daill rose to his feet. 'Then let's take a look around.'

They walked down to the next floor, where the carpets ended and an apparently endless rabbit warren of activity began. Telephones rang above the clack of typewriters and the chatter of adding machines. One glass-walled section held a battery of teletype machines, another housed a section of computer hardware.

'Home and domestic departments,' explained Daill, striding along. 'The paperwork side of banking. One could say the only time actual cash is seen here is on payday.'

They continued down, floor by floor, Daill continuing his running commentary. On the security side, the bank operated much as Thane had expected. Scottish banks seldom spent money on night-alarm or guard systems. They pinned their faith on the strength of their safes. By day, foot-operated alarms behind the counters were the main line of defence.

'Your task would be to alter that,' declared Daill. 'Photo-electric devices, closed-circuit cameras – we're ready to consider any overall project.'

'Why the change?' queried Thane.

Daill grimaced. 'A bitter lesson. Our sister bank in England lost a lot of money in two daytime raids. We wouldn't like it to happen here.'

They reached the ground floor, glanced at the public area, and turned along a corridor. Daill opened a door.

'Foreign Department,' he explained. 'Half the work here is keeping track of international exchange rates – particularly these days.'

They began walking between the desks. A figure heading towards them started to edge clear, but Daill saw him first.

'Manneson –'

The figure stopped and Thane fought down a start of surprise. It was the slim, fair-haired youngster he'd last seen lying in the alleyway outside the Lombok Club. Now he wore a plain, dark business suit. But the whole right side of his mouth was puffed and swollen around a deep cut.

'Sir?' The youngster barely glanced at Thane and gave no sign of recognition. It had been dark in that alleyway.

'Your face – what happened?' demanded Daill.

'I – I slipped and fell on the snow last night, sir.' A hand went up to the cut and touched it gently. 'I'm afraid it's pretty much of a mess.'

'Quite.' The banker frowned a little, then became heavily parental. 'Well, it can't be helped, Jim. But – ah – keep out of sight of the customers for a little while. Bad image projection. Right?'

'Yes, sir.' Manneson side-stepped as they moved on.

'What's his job?' queried Thane mildly.

'Young Manneson?' Daill waved a hand around. 'Junior clerk here, in the Foreign Department. At his stage it's dull work, but still important. He's one of our better lads.'

'Been with you for long?'

'About four years I think. Transferred to head office a couple of years back, not long before he got married.'

'Do you help junior staff financially – to set up house, I mean?' Thane chose his words carefully. 'Interest-free loans for house purchase, that sort of thing?'

'Yes. More or less interest-free, anyway. I approved one for Manneson – oh, a year ago. He bought a flat somewhere around Westpark.' Daill stopped at a blank-faced door, pressed a button to one side, and the door slid open. An iron grille behind it lay unlocked and a flight of steps led below.

They went down, into a world of bare concrete and harsh tube-lights. Another, heavier iron grille barred their way, and this one was locked. On the other side, a shirt-sleeved clerk rose from his desk, pulled a lever, and the grille rumbled back.

'And the end of the tour,' said Daill proudly. 'Over there – our strong-room. What do you think of it?'

Across the basement, like the opened breech-block of some enormous gun, the vast armoured door of the strong-room lay open. Inside, brightly lit, was a cavernous space the depth of a two-car garage.

'Made by Webb and Maber, fire-proof, bomb-proof, flood-proof – and very much thief-proof,' declared the banker. 'No security problem here, eh?'

Thane nodded, studying the door. 'Combination time-lock – and keys?'

'Four systems, each interdependent. The door's power-operated, weighs three tons on its own. According to Webb and Maber's people, it just might be blown open – but the kind of charge needed would bring down the whole damned building.'

'I wouldn't like to try.' Thane glanced around. The basement had a furnace room in one corner, a smaller, open furnace nearby, some odd bits and pieces of machinery, and rank upon rank of filing cabinets.

Daill looked at his watch. 'Well, I've another appointment. But that gives you a rough idea of things, eh? And I'll look forward to Thursday. We're hoping you'll say "yes".'

They went back up the steps and through the Foreign Department. Manneson was at one of the desks and didn't bother to look up as they passed. At the start of the public area Patterson Daill shook hands again before he headed off towards the elevator.

With plenty to think about, Thane walked slowly towards the main door. His mind was a jumble. What Daill had said about the job. What it could mean. And, coming through everything, the face of that fair-haired clerk.

He reached the revolving door, pushed his way through, and collided with someone coming in.

'Hey .. .' The indignant grunt changed key. 'Ach, hello, Mr Thane!'

The man wore a steel-grey riot-helmet with a matching steel-grey uniform. Carrying a heavy leather cash bag in each hand, he'd a truncheon dangling from a leather belt. Thane smiled. Until he retired, Donny MacBain had been a points duty cop in the Central Division.

'What's this, Donny?' he asked, thumbing at the uniform. 'Joined someone's private army?'

The ex-cop eased his grip on the bags. 'I've a wee part-time job, cash escort wi' a security outfit. Here's the boss coming now.'

Thane looked past him. A heavy sheepskin jacket over his grey lounge suit, Josh Barbar was coming towards them with a smaller cash bag swinging from his right hand. Barbar saw him at the same moment. The thin, copper-haired figure hesitated in mid-stride and the eyes widened a fraction behind the rimless glasses. Then he came on, smiling a greeting. 'Strayed from your area again, Chief Inspector? Things too quiet for you over in Millside?'

'We've enough to keep us going,' said Thane good-humouredly. 'I'm over on personal business.'

'Then there's no trouble inside?' Barbar's manner eased.

'If there is, they didn't tell me.' A small truck with the words 'Barbar Security' on the door panels was parked across the street, another uniformed man behind the wheel. 'Helping out, Mr Barbar?'

'For today,' agreed Barbar. 'We guarantee a three-man crew on cash runs and one of the regulars is off sick.' He glanced at MacBain. 'Take your load in, Donny – I'll follow on.'

The man nodded and ambled through the bank door.

'You mentioned this cash-transit sideline last night,' said Thane casually. 'Being kept busy?'

'Right now I'm losing money on it. But it's developing – given time, I may need a full-time crew.' Barbar grinned. 'Like Harry Freeman said, I may be looking for men. An ex-detective might do.'

'I'll try to remember,' said Thane dryly.

'Just a joke,' qualified Barbar quickly. 'Maybe you won't believe it, but I once tried to become a cop. The first time I knew I needed glasses was when I failed the medical.'

'Some people would rate that an escape.' Thane nodded towards the bank. 'How often do your men make the trip to here?'

'Usually Mondays to Fridays, mornings only. Except sometimes we've a special evening run when a customer wants something dropped into the night safe.' Barbar hefted his bag and took a half-step forward. 'I'd better get this inside. But if you're interested in the setup, call in at the office anytime.'

'I might do that,' agreed Thane.

As Barbar went into the bank, Thane reached into his pocket and located the car keys. Then he changed his mind and stayed where he was. Moments later Donny MacBain came out and he moved to intercept him.

'Enjoying life, Donny?'

'Add this wee job to my police pension and things are fine, Mr Thane.' They began walking together towards the parked security truck and the man grimaced slightly. 'Mind you, he wanted me on the debt-collectin' side but I didn't want that.'

'What's he like?'

'As a boss?' MacBain sucked his lips thoughtfully. 'Talks big at times, an' he can give you a funny feelin' you're a bit of a mug. But the money's good.'

They reached the truck. The driver's face was vaguely familiar, almost certainly another ex-cop. Thane said goodbye and returned to his car.

He reached Millside Division minutes after eleven, sneaked in through the station's rear entrance, and looked around almost guiltily as he entered the C.I.D. room. The tempo of activity seemed normal enough.

Once in his office he tossed his hat and coat aside and moved towards his desk. Before he got there the door swung open again and Phil Moss came in, the makings of a scowl on his face.

'Get what you wanted done?' asked Moss with an unusual look of cordiality.

Thane nodded. 'More or less. What about here?'

'Nothing that's going to make you happy,' said Moss heavily. 'I traced those two telephone numbers I found at Cullen's place. The first belongs to someone called Manneson.'

'James Manneson, out in Westpark?' Thane's mouth tightened.

'Yes, but –' Moss's mouth fell open a little. 'You know him?'

'Just that he's a bank clerk, the same youngster I found in that alley. I saw him fifteen, maybe twenty minutes ago.'

'But I thought –' Moss stopped and shook his head. 'Never mind. You're not going to like the rest of it. The other number is your bookie pal Freeman's home. And it just happens he's been on the phone twice since you left. He says he wants to see you out there – and that it's urgent.'

Chapter Four

Cullen with Harry Freeman's telephone number – it didn't make sense. Colin Thane gnawed his lip, instincts rejecting the situation, conscious that the whole fluid state of the case could be on the brink of pouring out of control.

Standing beside the crime map, Moss made an apologetic noise. 'There may be a simple enough reason, Colin.'

'There's got to be,' said Thane greyly. 'If there isn't, why would Harry steer me on to Cullen?' One hand beat a rapid, thoughtful tattoo on the desk. 'Let's take care of the bank clerk first. Where's Beech?'

'On an early lunch break. He went round the corner for a beer.'

'Then get him back and send him out to Westpark,' instructed Thane. 'Tell him we want anything he can dig up on this Manneson character's home life. I want him to try neighbours, the postman, shopkeepers, anyone – and I want it done quickly.'

'Another of his consumer surveys?' queried Moss. 'He'll want to know.'

Thane winced. Detective Constable Beech still had a smooth, comparatively innocent face. He also made a speciality of posing as a consumer-survey worker when it came to carrying out background probes. But the last time he'd gone almost too far – putting on a convincing act gathering opinions on the qualities of a nonexistent soap powder. Almost half the people he'd interviewed had promptly tried to get the product from their local stores – and the stores in turn had driven wholesalers nearly crazy by their demands for supplies.

'Make sure he picks a subject which won't land us in trouble. And he hasn't to go near Manneson's bank.'

'Which bank?' asked Moss innocently.

'Central Scotland's head office.' Thane glanced at his second-in-command sharply, but Moss's thin face showed only professional interest. 'You know what banks are like. If a member of staff lands anything worse than a parking ticket he's doomed for all time. Now, any word from Mac?'

'Just that he's still alive, still moving around, and that his feet are sore. What about Cullen? Does he stay down in the cells?'

Thane shook his head. Cullen seemed likely to be more valuable on the loose than in custody. 'I'll have him up here, then kick him out.'

'With a tail?'

'No tail,' said Thane positively. 'Cullen's a ned, but no fool. Until he's sure he isn't being followed he'll act as innocent as a ewe lamb. We'll leave him alone this afternoon, then pick things up and start watching from tonight.'

'And Harry Freeman?' asked Moss cautiously.

'We'll go there – both of us – once I've disposed of Cullen.' He had an afterthought as Moss began to amble towards the door. 'Phil, while we're at it we'll look in on the Alhambra warehouse. We'll do it on the way back.'

There was just enough time to make a couple of telephone calls. One was to Central Division. Yes, agreed the duty inspector, they'd certainly heard from Buddha Ilford on the matter of Sandy Lang. The buck-toothed bearded confidence-trickster was currently in a billiard hall a few streets away. His opponent happened to be a Central plain-clothes man, whose opposite number was watching near the door.

'You're organized,' congratulated Thane.

'Somebody's got to set an example to the other divisions,' said the Central inspector piously.

Thane described Central Division's efficiency and forebears in four short, pungently Scottish words and hung up. But he was still grinning as the switchboard connected him with the prison governor's office at Barlinnie Prison.

Barlinnie sat on a hill on the eastern edge of the city, a mouldering, antiquated fortress of a place usually crammed close to bursting point. But the governor usually managed to be patiently helpful.

'Andrew Fergan?' There was a brief rustle of papers. 'He's here until tomorrow, then he's due to be moved out to Peterhead – we're transferring a busload of new long-term men, normal routine.'

'How has Fergan taken it?'

'You can't sentence a man to life one day and expect him to be dancing around the next,' said the governor dryly. 'He was your case, wasn't he?'

'In a way he still is. I'd like to talk to him before he's moved,' said Thane.

'I'll tell him. But now he's convicted I can't force him.'

It was enough. Thane replaced the telephone and flipped the intercom switch. He heard the duty orderly answer.

'Bring Cullen up,' he ordered.

The cell-block turnkey, a broad, heavy-faced constable near to retiring age, brought Herb Cullen into the room within a couple of minutes.

'Leave him,' said Thane. 'And you can disinfect the cell if you want – we're letting him go.'

Herb Cullen's lips pulled back in a sneer as the turnkey

70

left. 'Discovered you've made a mistake, Thane? I told you I'd never heard of your damned warehouse.'

'Maybe – maybe not.' Thane leaned back in his chair, arms folded. 'I'm still interested in how you make such a fat living. Inspector Moss tells me you've quite a comfortable cave out at Claver Street.'

Cullen paled a little. 'Look, you'd no right –'

'We'd *every* right. We'd a search warrant. And take those hands off my desk. I like it to stay clean.' He rapped the words, the contempt in his voice striking anger in the ned's pale eyes.

Cullen controlled himself with an effort and took a slow step back. 'I can go?'

'Sooner the better. Your personal property's downstairs – pick it up.'

'I'll count the money, like I said.' Cullen produced a comb from his hip pocket and raised it to his mousy hair.

'Cullen' – Thane spoke softly – 'do you want my boot in your backside?'

The ned swallowed, slid the comb away, and backed out.

Monkswalk, the plushest section of Millside's area, was mainly broad lawns, ranch-style bungalows and an occasional outcrop of old stone mansion houses. Harry Freeman preferred the new. His home was a flat-roofed sprawl of glass and brick with a three-car garage to one side and a snow-covered space which was to be a swimming pool at the other.

'I'll never back another horse,' complained Moss bitterly as the duty C.I.D. car purred up a stretch of cleared gravel driveway. 'He doesn't stint himself, does he?'

'His old man sharpened knives from a barrow.' Thane leaned forward to their driver. 'Erickson, keep an ear on the radio. But don't drag me out unless it's vital.'

71

Erickson nodded and brought the Jaguar to a halt near a pair of matching M.G. sports coupés. Then he switched off and pushed his uniform cap back from his forehead, watching the others climb out.

Harry Freeman had named his house 'The Outsider' – with more than whimsy in mind. The front door was of sheet plate-glass, and as Thane and Moss walked towards it the dark-haired bookmaker appeared and swung it open.

'Come on in,' he invited. 'I've been twiddling my thumbs waiting.'

'I came as soon as I could.' Thane gestured Moss forward. 'You've met Phil?'

'A couple of times, a while back.' Freeman shivered despite his heavy wool sweater. 'Let's get this door closed and keep the heat in.'

They went inside, the warmth of the house hitting them like a wave. Freeman led the way into a small room which seemed to hold nothing but armchairs and ashtrays and waved an arm. 'Dump your coats anywhere. Like a drink?'

'Not right now, Harry.' Thane stripped off his coat and dropped it over the nearest armchair. Moss followed his example, glancing around with open curiosity. 'You said this was urgent.'

'I think so. From your point of view, anyway.' The bookmaker offered cigarettes. They took one each and accepted a light. 'Was that list of names I sent any use?'

'You didn't bring us out to ask that,' said Thane bluntly.

'No.' Freeman looked at him strangely for a moment then shrugged. 'I did a little bit of nosing around this morning, Colin. Bookies can sometimes get answers you wouldn't. Agreed?'

Thane nodded, but stayed silent.

'Anyway, I asked one or two people what Herb Cullen

was doing these days. Kept it on the line that I'd seen him at the Lombok Club last night.' He pursed his lips. 'People don't like talking about Cullen – it isn't reckoned too healthy. But he's in the money and has been for a while now. Enough to turn down a couple of propositions from – well, other people.'

'What propositions?' queried Moss.

Freeman shook his head. 'Sorry. That didn't interest me.'

Thane drew a deep, reluctant breath. 'Harry, just what *is* your interest?'

'Uh?' The bookmaker blinked. 'If you mean in this, call it for old times' sake.'

'Harry' – it came out as a sigh – 'we turned over Cullen's place this morning. We found a couple of telephone numbers. One of them was yours, this house.'

Freeman stared at him, flushing. 'I wondered what was wrong! So it's like that –'

'It was your number, Harry,' reminded Thane. 'Did he call you last night?'

'I've never spoken to him.' Freeman's lips formed a tight line for a moment. 'I didn't get home till about one this morning – part of the time I was at the office, drawing up that list for you. And before you ask, I haven't said to anyone that you want The Tallyman.' He swung on his heel, strode to the door, opened it, and called, 'Lil – can you come through?'

They heard an answer from somewhere in the house, then Harry Freeman's wife appeared. She was an attractive dark-haired woman built on generous lines, wearing slacks and a sweater.

She looked at Thane and smiled. 'Hello, Colin –'

'For the moment call him Chief Inspector,' said Freeman grimly. 'Lil, where were you last night?'

She frowned, a hand wearing a diamond like a pigeon's egg coming up to her lips. 'If it's something to do with the car –' she stopped and shook her head. 'I was here. I didn't go out.'

'When did I get home?'

'Your usual Monday – about one o'clock this morning.'

Freeman nodded. 'One more thing, Lil. Did anyone phone when I was out?'

'Oh.' Both hands were up now. 'Harry, I'm sorry – was it important?'

Moss stepped between them. 'You mean somebody did call, Mrs Freeman?'

She nodded. 'But – well, I forgot to tell Harry. I'd had a long day, and –'

'Who was it?' asked Freeman.

'Nobody I've ever heard before.' She looked from one face to the other, concern in her voice. 'He called twice, the first time just before midnight, then about half an hour after. But he didn't give a name, just said he wanted to speak to Harry.' Her nose wrinkled expressively. 'He didn't sound like a friend. I thought he was probably one of Harry's punters.'

The bookmaker gave a long sigh. 'Thanks, Lil.' He glanced at Thane, saw him shake his head, and propelled her gently towards the door. 'I'll tell you about it later.'

Thane waited till the door had closed. 'Harry –'

'If we were still kids I'd land you one in the guts,' declared Freeman. He scowled, but it gave way to a wry smile. 'I know you had to find out. And I'd better admit it – I'm not just doing this for old times' sake. You've got the Fergan business on your conscience. Well, maybe I've got something the same. I didn't help you first time, back when it began, because I didn't know much and I didn't really care.'

'But there's a difference now?' queried Moss, interested.

The bookmaker gave a fractional nod. 'Clean neds I can tolerate. But The Tallyman plays dirty. I heard a story – no names with it, but I can trust where it came from. Somebody had the pressure put on. The man had a bad heart, but that made no difference to The Tallyman. So' – he shrugged – 'the client kept being pressured and couldn't take it. He collapsed and died.'

'That's all?' Thane had a strange feeling there was something more involved, despite Freeman's obvious sincerity.

'For me, it's enough.' Freeman brushed the aspect aside with a wave of his hand. 'Colin, there's one thing really new I have heard, and it's positive. Does the Housewives' Special mean anything?' He saw their bewilderment. 'That's one of the collection runs, for housewives who've landed on his book – usually the husbands don't know. The women are told to travel on a certain bus route, same time each week. The collector is aboard waiting.'

'Which route?'

'I'm trying to find out.'

'Not any more.' Thane laid a heavy emphasis on the words. 'Harry, remember those phone calls. Cullen would probably have called again today if we hadn't shoved him in a cell. Somebody's on to you – don't ask me how. But you're being warned off the course.'

'By Cullen?' Freeman showed his contempt.

'He hasn't the brains to do it on his own. And you've Lil to consider. So I'm saying it now. No more. Stay clear of it.' He paused long enough to let the warning sink in, then looked around. 'A while back you made noises about a drink. Where's the stuff hidden this time?'

'Simple.' Freeman chuckled as he pressed a button. A motor whirred and a miniature bar swung out of what looked like the fireplace.

Moss blinked. 'I'll be damned!'

'That's what the character said who paid for it,' said Freeman solemnly. 'He lost out on a photo-finish. What'll it be?'

'Gin and tonic – without the gin,' said Moss wearily. His

75

ulcer kicked – in agreement or derision, he wasn't sure which.

Constable Erickson was almost asleep when they returned to the duty car. But he straightened up as they climbed aboard, stifled a yawn, and reported the radio had been quiet.

'The Alhambra warehouse next,' Thane told him.

As the car crunched back down the driveway they had a glimpse of Harry Freeman standing at one of the house windows.

'Quite a character,' mused Moss after a spell. 'And he doesn't scare easily.'

'That's his trouble.' Thane sank back against the seat cushions, far from happy. 'Phil, take it Cullen was going to warn him off. Why? Just because he saw us together at that club?'

Moss shook his bead. 'Somebody tipped them.'

'And I can guess who.' It came from Thane's lips like a curse. 'Rab Hayes.'

'Millside's favourite money-lender?' Moss sniffed derisively. 'He hasn't got the guts.'

'He's more scared of them than he is of us. It *has* to be Hayes. At that stage there was no one else involved outside of our own men – well, maybe that's not one hundred per cent accurate. Mac had begun asking questions out at the Turkish Raven. But I'm damned if I can see the word coming from there.'

'It's unlikely,' admitted Moss. 'Let's see how it would go. Hayes tipped off Cullen –'

'Tipped off someone,' corrected Thane. 'Then Cullen was put to work.'

'After being told at the Lombok Club?'

'Then or later. Cullen wasn't keen to tell us where he'd gone from the Lombok. And it ties in, Phil. Having young Manneson's phone number on the same envelope probably

76

comes down to calling and warning him to keep his mouth shut.'

'I wonder what our little bank clerk's done –' Moss broke off. They were turning into King Street, the car's tyres churning through uncleared slush. The gaunt shape of the Alhambra warehouse loomed ahead. 'How long here?'

'Just enough to keep the management happy.' Thane put it no higher. The Millside detectives working on the break-in weren't likely to have overlooked anything.

The warehouse manager's name was Bissett, a glum, worried individual with a face to match, and he showed them around the building with a spluttering anger. The raiders had squeezed in through a rear window, then cut a burglar alarm on the main door before smashing the lock.

Traces of fingerprint powder were still around, showing where the Scientific Bureau team from Headquarters had been at work. That was routine. But in city crime, any crook would agree, a man still stupid enough to leave fingerprints deserved to be caught.

From the main warehouse Bissett led the way to a small cubicle of an office on the upper floor. It smelled of damp and the floor hadn't been swept.

'We're lodging a protest, a protest direct to the Chief Constable,' he snapped bitterly. 'The police knew this was going to happen. You even had a watch on the place for a time. But nobody warned us. We want to know why.'

'Who told you we'd been watching?' demanded Thane sharply.

'A detective. One of the pair who dragged me out of bed after it happened.'

Phil Moss saw the look which crossed the Millside chief's face and said a quick prayer for the unfortunate d.c. who'd made that mistake.

'We'd – well, certain information,' agreed Thane cautiously. 'But nothing definite, Mr Bissett. If we kept permanent watch on every place we're told may be done we'd a need an army.'

Bissett snorted. 'Well, this bunch must have been watching too. The transistor sets have been here for long enough. But the colour TVs – hell, man, they only arrived yesterday. I haven't got the invoices yet!'

'You were asked to draw up a list of employees, Mr Bissett,' prodded Moss gently. 'Is it ready?'

'Waste of time. Everyone's been with us for years.' The man grumbled on but opened his desk and shoved an envelope at them. Moss put it in his pocket.

'That's all for now, Mr Bissett.' Thane moved towards the door. 'We'll keep in touch.'

'You'd better,' warned the warehouse manager bleakly. 'We're going to take this all the way.'

They went back to the car. Thane stopped beside it, glanced at Moss, shrugged, and lit a cigarette.

'Food,' suggested Moss hopefully. 'It's a long time since I ate.' He could have added that his right foot felt damp and cold. The shoe must be letting in.

Thane glanced at his watch and nodded. 'Might as well – but we'll make it quick, then split up. You take Rab Hayes and shake some truth out of him. I'll check how Beech is getting on with our bank clerk's home life.'

'And this "Housewives' Special" business?'

'If there's anything in it, Harry Freeman will find out.'

'But you told him –'

Thane nodded grimly. 'I know. But what you tell him and what he does are two different things.'

Detective Constable Michael Beech was enjoying himself. He was using his Mini, which meant mileage allowance. He was using his own initiative, and he was young enough for this to be a particular satisfaction. Best of all, people around the lower-middle-income sector called Westpark seemed to really enjoy telling him which television programmes they'd like to see dropped from the small screen.

He settled back behind the wheel, took a bite from a slab of chocolate, and glanced at the fake census notebook he'd been using. Beech chuckled. The last entry was an elderly spinster who wanted more sunshine in her weather forecasts. But she'd been useful. Her flat overlooked the one occupied by Jim Manneson and his wife.

Beech took out his police notebook, began writing, then jerked round in surprise as the passenger door clicked open.

'Lock it next time. I could have had a gun.' Colin Thane squeezed himself aboard the little car, knocked the worst of the snow from his feet, and slammed the door shut again. 'You took some finding.'

'Sorry, sir.' Beech glanced around, swallowing the last of the chocolate.

'The duty car's a few streets away,' said Thane dryly. 'I thought you'd prefer that. Any luck?'

'Yes, sir.' Beech grinned. 'Manneson arrived home for lunch a little while back. He comes at the same time every day. He's still up there. I spoke to his wife about an hour back – I was in the flat. She's quite a piece of homework.'

Thane raised an eyebrow but said nothing.

The grin died. 'I did all the flats in her block, and –'

'And you're wasting time,' said Thane wearily.

Beech tried again. 'Well, her name's Irene, she's twenty – a year younger than Manneson. She's the original dumb blonde except that she's a redhead. And the house looks good, too good for a junior bank clerk.'

'Money worries?'

'I'd say plenty, and the reason's easy enough. Her sales resistance is nil – she's a door-to-door man's dream.'

'The gambling type?'

79

'No, sir. I asked if she liked horse racing. She'd ban it – says she thinks betting is immoral.'

'Her husband doesn't.' Thane glanced at him. 'But you think it's the girl?'

'Who's running up debts?' Beech nodded. 'The neighbours say so. They've had a washing machine and a lounge-suite repossessed, they owe every shopkeeper in the district, and the postman says most of their mail looks like final-demand notices. The locals feel pretty sorry for him.'

There was a tap on the passenger window. They looked round. An elderly woman in a red cape and rubber boots waggled a hand in greeting, smiled at Beech, and headed off down the street.

'A friend?' queried Thane.

'People remember me,' said Beech modestly. 'That's Mrs MacPhee. She thinks Children's TV is produced by sadists.'

'Children are sadists anyway,' said Thane absently. 'All right, start this thing and take me round to the duty car. Then head back for Millside. Inspector Moss can probably use you somewhere.'

'Yes, sir.' Deflated, Beech reached for the ignition key.

'Beech' – Thane eyed him, frowning – 'why did you want to be a cop?'

'Me?' The younger man scratched his head. 'I didn't, sir. It just happened that way.'

He started the car and they jerked away. Thane directed him through the turnings until the police Jaguar appeared parked ahead. The Jaguar's headlamps flashed once – recognition and a sure sign that Erickson was anxious about something.

'Wait,' said Thane as the Mini drew in. The d.c. nodded.

Erickson had a radio-message pad on his knee when Thane clambered in beside him. The uniformed man tore off the top sheet and passed it over.

'Came about two minutes ago, sir,' he said tonelessly. 'I was thinking of trying to find you.'

Thane read the message once again, hardly believing it at first.

'Timed 15:05 from Control for attention Chief Inspector Thane. Proceed City Mortuary re body of Herbert Cullen. Message ends.'

His stomach felt suddenly cold and empty. Slowly, carefully, he handed the message slip back and moistened his lips.

'Tell Beech to follow us,' he said quietly.

In the old days, Glasgow's city mortuary was a shed on a patch of waste ground – and pathologists had to contend with the noise of the city's police pipe-band, who held their practice sessions outside. But the new mortuary, a single-storey brick building, was a quiet, antiseptic place well insulated from the outside world.

Beech close at his heels, Colin Thane followed an attendant down a short, cream-tiled corridor. The man gestured towards a cubicle, muttered he was busy, and hurried off.

'Come on in, Colin.' Immaculate as ever, but with a white overall protecting his pin-striped suit, a familiar figure waited by the window. Doc Williams, the city's senior police surgeon, greeted him with a briskly cheerful air. He wasn't alone. A Central Division detective, distinctly unhappy, stood in the corner furthest away from the marble-topped table and its sheet-covered figure.

Thane nodded in greeting, then glanced towards the table. 'Is this –'

'Uh-huh. One Herbert Cullen.' Doc Williams twisted a grin. 'It goes like a poem. "Our city is now one ned less – he fell in front of an underground express."'

The Central man winced disapprovingly, but Thane was more used to Doc Williams' ways. The police surgeon treated death as everyday business and wore an acid humour like battered armour.

'Well, maybe it doesn't scan too well,' confessed Williams. 'But that's more or less what happened. Sergeant Franks has been handling inquiries. If you want to take a look, I've tidied things up a little.'

'I'd better.'

'Right.' The smile gone from his face, Doc Williams quietly lifted one corner of the sheet. Sergeant Franks studiously looked the other way. Standing beside Thane, D. C. Beech made a sudden retching noise and disappeared from the cubicle.

'I don't blame him.' The police surgeon replaced the sheet. 'It is Cullen?'

Thane drew a deep breath, shaken by what he'd seen. 'I think so. But in that mess –' He turned to the Central man. 'What happened?'

'We'd an emergency call to St. Enoch underground station just after two p.m., a report a man had gone under a train.' Sergeant Franks rubbed a hand over his face at the recollection. 'It took a while to get him out. Then a while longer to get identification – until we found a Millside Division receipt in his pocket. The usual personal effects thing, sir. From there, our duty inspector decided you'd better know.'

'Chief Inspector Thane's real interest lies in another question, I'd imagine,' mused Doc Williams. 'Did he jump, did he fall, or was he pushed. Right, Colin?'

Thane nodded. 'Any pointers, Sergeant?'

Sergeant Franks shook his head. 'The platform was jammed with people, sir. We've one or two witnesses, but all they say is that Cullen seemed to fall forward just as the train came in.'

'And don't expect much from me,' warned Doc Williams, hitching his thumbs in the overall pockets. 'If some-

82

body shot or stabbed him first, fine. But otherwise this is an off season for miracles.'

'We're running a fingerprint check to make sure of identification,' volunteered Sergeant Franks. 'Eh . . . did he matter much, sir?'

'He mattered a lot.' Thane pursed his lips. 'Who was near him when it happened?'

'The best we've got are a couple of office girls who were standing a few feet away. They think he was talking to someone – another man. But they can't give any description.'

He had to accept it. When a man fell in front of a train people concentrated on the man – not on who'd been on the same edge of the crowded platform.

'You'll do what you can, Doc?'

'I always try,' said the police surgeon in a slightly hurt voice. 'I'll be in touch.'

Thane left him, looking for Beech as he went back along the corridor. The staff-room door was open and when he reached it he stopped short, surprised. Beech was inside, smoking a cigarette, his face still pale. Straddling a chair beside him, Phil Moss glanced up first.

'Well, Colin?'

'What the devil brought you here?' asked Thane, going in.

'I heard the radio call about Cullen,' said Moss easily. 'And I wanted to get hold of you.'

'Sir' – Beech took a fractional step forward – 'I'm sorry about back there.'

'Don't be. Worry when you get the other way.' Thane swung back to his second-in-command. 'You got Rab Hayes?'

'No. His place was closed – the neighbours say he always takes Tuesday afternoon off.' Moss dismissed the money-lender. 'Anyway, I thought I'd go round to the house addresses on the Alhambra staff list, just looking from the outside –'

'Phil –'

Moss ignored the interruption. 'I found company at the third house. Sergeant MacLeod was there with his w.p.c. The same address was on his list. One of the ones you got from Harry Freeman!'

Thane whistled softly and hopefully. 'Who is it?'

'A storeman, name of Patrick Lucas. I told MacLeod to collect him from work.' Moss glanced at his watch. 'He should be at Millside by now, waiting.'

'Good.' Thane thought for a moment. 'Phil, take Beech and get out to Cullen's place. Search it again, bring in anything you find, and ask the Scientific bunch to go over it too. Check at Hayes' place on the way back. If he's there, bring him in whether he likes it or not. I'll see you when you get back.'

Moss nodded, gestured to Beech, and they headed for the door. As they left, Thane crossed to the telephone lying on a corner table. A directory lay beside it and he flicked through until he found Harry Freeman's home number. He dialled, heard the number ring out, and waited. There was no reply. He tried the bookie's office number next, and had an answer on the second ring.

'Mr Freeman?' The girl on the other end of the line answered with a bored unconcern. 'Sorry. There's no racing today. We're not expecting him in. Can I take a message?'

'Tell him to call Millside and that it's urgent.' Biting his lip, Thane replaced the telephone.

So far he'd kept the thought to himself. But it was there, screaming for attention. For the moment Herb Cullen was Central Division's pigeon – but people like Cullen just didn't fall under subway trains by accident.

More likely someone had decided Cullen was a risk, a risk best disposed of before he became too troublesome.

And if Cullen had been a risk, then Harry Freeman might shade his way into the same category.

Once more he lifted the telephone and dialled the bookmaker's home number. Again there was no reply. Grimfaced, Thane laid down the receiver and went out.

Winter dusk was giving way to night as he reached Millside. The snow had begun again, light but persistent. Heading for his office, Thane saw Sergeant MacLeod waiting patiently to one side and beckoned him along.

'You collected this storeman, Mac?'

'Yes, sir.' MacLeod closed the door, shutting out the noise of the main office. 'He – ah – didn't seem too surprised.'

'Did you tell him why he was wanted?'

MacLeod shook his head. 'Inspector Moss said lift and bring – I said nothing.'

'Good.' There were two teleprinter messages on the desk and he glanced at them quickly.

Scientific Branch confirmed that the truck found abandoned in Eastern Division had been used on the Alhambra job. The fragments of broken crate found aboard had been positively identified. But they'd found nothing else.

Central Division were keeping their watch on Sandy Lang. But if the former confidence trickster was one of The Tallyman's collectors he seemed in no hurry to get to work. The last report placed him loafing around a shopping arcade.

Thane pushed the messages aside. 'I'll see this storeman in a minute, Mac. What about the rest on your list?'

MacLeod pondered a moment. 'Some don't count, sir. They're just welching on bets. But five at least are up to their necks in debt.'

'Any pattern?'

'Hard to say.' MacLeod rasped a hand along his chin.

'Except – well, three families have had the debt-collection agencies in, trying to organize repayment.'

'The Barbar crowd?' The question was out almost before he realized it.

'For two of them, yes.' The sergeant frowned. 'Out of those two, one is a real possible. I got to the husband – he shut up like a clam when I asked about outside loans.' He sucked his teeth gently. 'He was one o' the names I got at the Turkish Raven last night.'

The grind, the routine, the monotony of doorbell ringing was beginning to work. Satisfied, Thane nodded. 'And our storeman, Mac – has he been worked on yet by the Barbar Agency?'

'I don't know,' confessed MacLeod. 'I'd just started questioning his wife when Inspector Moss arrived.'

He sent MacLeod to fetch the man, and there was time enough to try Harry Freeman's house again. The same steady ringing with no reply continued until he hung up.

Patrick Lucas, storeman, was small, worried and parrot-nosed. He had thin, greying hair, was still in his working garb, and moistened his lips nervously as he took the chair opposite Thane's desk.

'Ever been in trouble before, Lucas?' asked Thane crisply. 'Police-type trouble?'

'Never. I haven't – I mean –' Lucas swallowed hard. 'I just got hustled here an' –'

'And now we're going to tell you why.' Face expressionless, Thane glanced at MacLeod. 'Notebook.'

'Sir.' MacLeod made a flourishing production of dragging out book and pencil.

'As it's your first time, Lucas, I'll explain,' said Thane with a lazy emphasis. 'Before we charge anyone we caution – tell them they don't need to say anything but that if they do we can use it later. After that there are technicalities. But they're our worries.' He looked at Lucas for a moment and shook his head. 'The Alhambra warehouse – well, you certainly picked a big enough beginning.'

The man's eyes widened. 'Mister –'

'We'll get started,' said Thane, the words like a whip-crack. 'Sergeant –'

'Will you listen, mister!' It came like an anguished squeak. 'You've got it wrong. I'm – I'm the one who tipped you off. Me' – he tapped his chest hard and fast – 'me.'

'You?' Thane sighed and leaned back. 'When?'

'Over – over a week ago. An' you put cops on watchin' the place.'

'Somebody phoned,' agreed Thane. 'But he wouldn't give a name. And he didn't bother to tell us the job was being put back because those TV sets hadn't arrived.'

'Aye. But – but I couldn't risk phoning again.' Lucas still resembled a parrot, but one which was moulting. 'Still, it makes a difference, right?'

On cue, MacLeod cleared his throat. 'You'll know who they were then, Mr Lucas?'

The storekeeper looked down at his feet and shook his head.

'Lucas – I'm talking to you.' Thane waited until the man's gaze met his own. 'How much do you owe?' He sensed a gathering stubbornness. 'Lucas, the sergeant saw your wife.'

Alarm flared in the watery eyes. 'She's –'

'Not involved. We know that. Just like we know about The Tallyman.' He made a smooth transfer to a friendlier mood. 'Now let's start right at the beginning. When did things get to the stage that the debt-collection agency moved in?'

The man shrugged. 'Six, maybe seven, months back.'

'The Barbar Agency?' Thane accepted the answering nod and kept on with the faintest pause. 'And how long after that till The Tallyman's agent made contact?'

87

'I' – the man licked his lips and gave in – 'a couple o' months.'

He'd started. The rest came easily enough. Lucas had been approached in a bar and offered a loan – twenty pounds at first, then another twenty which he needed for rent money. But soon the interest payments, the inevitable twenty-five per cent per week, reared into the reckoning.

'So they leaned on you,' paraphrased Thane. 'Hard?'

Lucas nodded, his lips tight.

'Then they offered you a deal. That they'd wipe out the debt if you'd tell them when there was a really good load due at the warehouse – tell them that and how to collect it?'

'Why ask if you know?' It came like a groan.

Thane offered him a cigarette and a light. Lucas drew greedily on the smoke, listening hard now.

'It could make a difference if you helped us now, Mr Lucas. Who collected for The Tallyman?'

'The same fella I met in the bar. He – he's thin, with a beard.'

'And teeth like a rabbit,' nodded Thane. 'His name's Lang. Anyone else?'

'Just the two who beat me up,' said the storeman bitterly. 'Young neds wi' steel-toed boots. An' they used them. But it was dark – I didn't see their faces. After that, I did what they wanted.'

'And they always contacted you through Lang?'

'Mostly.' He swallowed. 'But there was another of them – he'd phone me at the warehouse. He's the one I told the television sets had arrived.'

'Nothing more?' Thane saw the answer and was satisfied. 'And you'd be prepared to give evidence about this – all of it – in court?'

'If –' The storeman read the warning in Thane's eyes and nodded quickly. 'Yes.'

'Good.' Thane glanced at MacLeod. 'He's yours, Mac. Get a statement signed. And hold him for now.'

Lucas was led out. Before the door had properly closed, Thane had Andrew Fergan's case file and was thumbing through the statements which mattered. None mentioned the Barbar Agency. But that could be because the question hadn't been asked.

He slammed the file shut. The picture was beginning to focus, with one unexpected detail in the foreground.

Unexpected? No, he'd blundered, hadn't realized what could be meant when Rab Hayes first hinted The Tallyman didn't always seek cash. He cursed the money-lender's obtuse way of trying to play both ends for the sake of his middle-position safety. He had cost them time – time and maybe more.

The Barbar Agency's case sheets must be one of the primary sources from which The Tallyman selected his victims. Equally certain, some victims were hand-picked because of occupation, then forced to help from the inside in planned robberies.

Next on the list? Well, it might be a certain pale-faced young bank clerk whose wife couldn't resist a bargain. And that could mean the target was the Bank of Central Scotland – in which Colin Thane now possessed an uneasy, personal interest.

He shut his eyes for a moment at the thought. But there were more immediate matters. He reached for the telephone again.

This time Harry Freeman's home number rang only three times before a woman's voice answered.

He gave a grunt of relief. 'Lil? It's Colin Thane. Is Harry with you?'

'No.' She sounded slightly concerned. 'I've been out shopping and he's been away too. But – well, I expected him back by now. Unless the doctor kept him waiting.'

'Which doctor?'

'Norman Milne, the heart specialist.' She sighed. 'No, I don't suppose you'd know. He goes regularly, but he hasn't told anyone. It was long enough before I found out. Harry's got some idiotic notion people would treat him like an invalid if word got out.'

'He certainly didn't say anything to me.' Which was typically stubborn, added Thane mentally. 'Lil, I'll try there. But if he comes home soon, tell him to call me straight away.'

She agreed and hung up. Thane thumbed the receiver rest until the station switchboard answered, told them to get him Doctor Milne's consulting rooms, and lit a cigarette while he waited.

The heart specialist's receptionist answered the call and he asked for Freeman.

'Mr Freeman's been here, Chief Inspector,' she agreed immediately. 'But he left about a couple of hours ago. I was just saying to Doctor Milne that Mr Freeman's M.G. was still outside, that he hadn't come back for it –'

'Come back from where?' Thane tensed.

She laughed. 'Don't ask me why – it was none of my business. But he made a joke about going for a bus run. He wanted to know if we'd mind the car being left parked outside.'

He drew a deep breath. 'Which bus? It could be important.'

'That's easy,' said the receptionist confidently. 'Mr Freeman said he had to get the three-forty p.m. bus for Fallside. I remember because that's the local 238 service, the one I use to get home – there's a bus every half hour. Chief Inspector –'

'Yes?'

'There's nothing wrong, is there? I mean, Mr Freeman's one of my favourite patients.'

'I don't know. Not yet.' He hung up.

From the city centre to Fallside was only a twenty-

90

minute journey. Twenty minutes there, twenty minutes back – and Harry Freeman had been gone almost two hours.

Thane flipped the intercom switch and ordered the duty car to meet him at the front door. Seconds later he grabbed his coat and started on his way.

He reached the stairway to find Phil Moss coming up, Beech a few steps behind with Rab Hayes at his side.

'We found him,' said Moss cheerfully.

Thane barely glanced at the fat, wheezing money-lender. 'Leave him to Beech. Harry Freeman's in trouble.'

Moss stopped short, his lips framing a question. But Thane was already halfway down the stairs. He swung round and followed.

Chapter Five

The snow was coming down picture-book fashion as the duty car headed out, screen wipers slapping. It lay white on the rooftops but was a churned brown slush on the main roads, mess sprayed wide as tyres smacked the deeper pools.

Constable Erickson was at the wheel. He'd been told they had a rush job, which was enough. Blue warning-light flashing, headlamps blazing, he had his foot down and was enjoying himself. It was different at the rear. Phil Moss listened quietly as Thane sketched what had happened. He started to reach for the herbal cigarettes, changed his mind, took a bismuth tablet instead, and sucked it gently as he made his own contribution.

'We found Hayes easily enough this time. He was walking up to his front door – and believe me, right now he's scared.' Moss glanced at Thane, got no response, and carried on determinedly. 'Things were different at Herb Cullen's apartment. Somebody got there ahead of us.'

That got through. Thane frowned, steadied himself as the car took two lumbering trucks at a single sweep, and asked, 'You're sure?'

'Positive. The lock hadn't been forced, but the apartment had been turned over. The money was gone – and the gun.' Moss made an attempt at hopefulness. 'After what I did to the firing pin it won't be much good to anyone.

Anyway there's always the chance Cullen was carrying it —'

'Even Central Division would make a noise if they'd found a corpse packing a Beretta.' Thane hunched forward, peering ahead, cursing the night and the weather. 'You tried the neighbours?'

'Beech did, but got nowhere. The three wise monkeys would be nonstarters against those people.'

The shops and tenements had faded to neat terrace houses and occasional neon-bright filling stations. As traffic thinned and they left the city behind, the snow lay thicker.

Fallside was more a plan than a district. Someday it would be a dormitory community. For the moment it was one third residential, one third building sites, and the rest waste ground. The road became almost empty, bus-stop signs were wider spaced. At last their headlamps showed a grove of trees ahead, a bus bay and a telephone kiosk at their fringe.

'This is where they turn, sir.' Erickson let the car coast in. The tyres crunched on virgin snow as they stopped.

Two torches were clipped to the car's equipment shelf. Thane took one, tossed the other to Moss, and they climbed out as Erickson switched off the engine. Moss glanced at the trees, then at Thane, the question unspoken. Erickson joined them, pulling the hood of his dark nylon raincoat up over his uniform cap.

'We'll try the wood,' nodded Thane almost reluctantly. 'Space out – and careful how you go.' He led the way, torchbeam cutting the black shadows under the trees.

Shivering, plodding ankle-deep, Moss followed with Erickson on their right.

They hadn't far to go. A narrow path ran through the trees, a shortcut from the bus shelter to houses in the far background. Twenty yards in, a little to the right of the path, the low bulk of a gorse bush formed a windbreak. To one side, just beyond the bush, a huddled shape lay sprawled on the ground, snow-frosted, already beginning to blend into the surrounding white.

Moss's torchbeam found it first, a moment before Erickson reached the bush. They stopped, Moss shouted, and Thane came crashing over. Both torches swept the area. There was no sign of footprints. Thane nodded. Keeping to a tight single file, they went over.

Harry Freeman lay on his side, head twisted round, limbs bent as he'd fallen. His mouth was open and his eyes stared emptily in the torches' light.

Thane knelt and gently brushed the white crusting from his friend's face. There was no need to feel for a pulsebeat. Freeman was dead.

At last, he got to his feet and looked round.

'Where's Erickson?'

'Back at the car. I told him to radio in.' Moss had carefully restrained sympathy in his voice. 'Colin, I'm sorry.'

Thane nodded, tight-lipped. 'He always was a stubborn devil,' he said softly. 'More courage than sense – that was his trouble.'

'Aye.' Habit and routine made Moss check his watch. It was almost six p.m. Even with a fast turnout, the Scientific squad and the rest would need time to get through the rush-hour traffic. He swung his torch back to Freeman. 'What happened?'

'There's no wound – none I can see.' The words came clipped. Colin Thane would have given most things to find an outlet for the dull anger eating inside him. He escaped into the tasks that waited. 'See if Erickson has a blanket or something, Phil. And get on to Control. I want the crew who manned that bus – I don't give a damn what has to be done to find them.'

'Right.' Moss hesitated. 'What about you?'

'I'll check around for a spell.'

Moss started off, then looked back. Thane was still standing there. The tall, broad-shouldered figure was motionless, the torch switched off.

A cloud of powdered snow fell from a branch, hit Moss, and began melting down the back of his neck. He wiped it away, sighed, and headed for the radio.

The first help to arrive took the shape of two carloads of uniformed men from Millside Division. Thane used most of them to cordon off the cluster of trees and the bus bay, but sent a couple of men back down the road in a car with orders to turn any bus traffic short of the usual terminus.

All except one bus. Control had managed a fast check with the city Transport Department. The vehicle which had made the 3:40 run to Fallside on the 238 route was still operating with the same crew aboard. By timetable, it was now on its way out again from town.

A little later, when Moss came looking for him, Thane was back near the gorse bush, smoking a cigarette. A few feet away, snow was beginning to settle fast on the tarpaulin they'd used to cover Freeman.

'That's it for the moment,' reported Moss. 'Control say Dan Laurence is coming out.'

'Good.' Thane felt happier at the news. Superintendent Laurence, head of the Scientific Bureau, was a rough-tongued, white-haired bear of a man. But when Dan Laurence led his team on a job he stayed with it till the end. 'And the bus?'

'It should arrive pretty soon.' Moss wrapped his coat tighter around him. 'Let's get back to the car for a spell. You must be damned near frozen – I am.'

'In a minute.' Thane cupped one hand round the cigarette and it glowed bright for a moment. 'There's a trace of car tracks further down the road, Phil. I've had them covered with another of Erickson's tarpaulins. But look

95

around you. We left footprints coming through this stuff. Why no others – not even Harry's?'

'The snow –' began Moss.

'It isn't falling heavily enough for that – not in here under the trees,' said Thane impatiently. 'Someone brushed them out.'

'Or it looks that way,' qualified Moss. There were headlights on the road towards them, three vehicles in close convoy. 'Company – we'd better go meet them.'

The first of the three to pull in was a Headquarters car. Then came a red Rover 2000 with Doc Williams behind the wheel, followed by a big, sand-coloured van, the Scientific Bureau mobile laboratory.

The police surgeon gathered his bag from the passenger seat and came towards them accompanied by a familiar, shaggy-haired figure in an ancient sheepskin jacket. Dan Laurence was grumbling as they approached.

'You picked a hell o' a night to find this one, Colin,' complained the Bureau chief. 'Who is he?'

'A friend,' said Thane bluntly. 'And I didn't arrange the weather.'

Laurence glanced at him sharply. 'Sorry, man. I didn't know.' Snow was already beginning to coat his eyebrows. He brushed it away. 'Ach, damn the stuff – well, what's the picture?'

'While you're finding out I can get started,' declared Doc Williams with an unusual absence of humour. 'Phil –'

Moss nodded and they set off into the trees. Behind them, at the roadside, Laurence's men were already unloading equipment from the mobile lab.

It took about a minute for the Scientific Bureau chief to learn what he wanted.

'Everybody be careful where you put your great feet,' he bellowed to his squad. 'Stick to established tracks.' A finger stabbed. 'Tommy –'

96

'Sir?' A d.c. draped in cameras and flash equipment came forward.

'Leave the general views till later. We've car tracks under a tarp. Get some shots as they are. Jock – when he's done that use the blower and a paint aerosol on them. Then he can take more. Move to the body next and try the same drill round about. Some of the rest of you give him a hand with the tarps.' He swung back to Thane. 'Colin, there's a flask of coffee in the van. You look like you could use some – unless you prefer frostbite.'

'Later.' Thane pointed down the road. A bus was heading in their direction, the route number 238 clear on its indicator board. 'I've been waiting for this one.'

He was at the roadside when the bus slithered to a halt. It was a single-decker, the older type still operated by a two-man crew of driver and conductor, the driver isolated in his cab. Thane beckoned the driver to come round and swung himself aboard at the passenger door.

The conductor, a dark, small-featured Pakistani, rose from one of the front seats and eyed him with nervous uncertainty.

'Police,' said Thane shortly, looking around the empty bus. 'What's your name?'

'I am Ussef Ali, sair.' The conductor clasped both hands tightly over his ticket machine, as if to gain comfort. 'And my driver –'

'I'll do my own answerin', Ali.' The voice was Glasgow-Irish. The bus driver, thin, middle-aged, came aboard with a stub of cigarette dangling from one corner of his mouth.

'I'm Dave Forgan. An' I'd like to know what the pink hell's goin' on. We're stopped by cops, an' wee Ali here has to heave the passengers out an' –'

'We've a dead man in that wood,' snapped Thane. 'We think he was one of your passengers on the last run.'

97

'Our flamin' luck!' It came like a groan. 'Mister, we're due off shift in half an hour.'

'You *were*,' corrected Thane, switching back to the Pakistani. 'How busy were you on the 3:40 trip out?'

Thin shoulders shrugged under the green Transport jacket. 'Not too much, sair. Women mostly – they shop, then go home.'

'Did you carry a man – tall, dark hair – to the terminus?'

The conductor hesitated and his driver grunted a protest.

'Look, mate, that's askin' a lot. Ali's a Paki – an' you know how it goes. Pakis pretty well look all the same to me. We probably look all the same to them.'

A touch of amusement quivered to Ali's lips. 'Dave is wrong, sair – though he tries to help. Yes, there was such man. He sat at the back. I remember he did not know how much to pay. He was a cheerful man.'

Thane nodded grimly. 'How many were still on the bus when it reached here?'

'A few – perhaps ten.' The conductor shook his head. 'I am sorry, sair. I cannot remember. We pay little attention.'

'Then did you notice another man, one who spoke to different women passengers, perhaps changed seats – anything like that?'

Ali's manner stiffened. 'I would not allow such happenings on my bus, sair. It is against Transport Department rules!'

His driver chuckled. 'Look, if it helps, there was a car parked up the road a bit when we pulled in. Somebody on the bus was bein' met.'

Thane brought him over to the door. 'Where these men are now?'

'Aye.'

'Did you see a man going towards it?'

'Nope.' The driver spat out what was left of the cigarette. 'It was a woman – she was wrapped up in a duffel coat but she'd nice legs. That's why I remember – I still had the headlights on.'

'Did anyone follow her – or did you see what kind of car it was?' asked Thane quickly.

Slowly, the driver shook his head. 'Sorry, mister. Like Al says, we don't pay much attention. It might have been a sports car – but I couldn't be sure of anythin' else.'

Patiently, Thane took them through their stories again. He could get no further, but what they said fitted.

It was straightforward sense for The Tallyman to use a woman to collect from women – even if he probably had a male 'minder' installed elsewhere on the bus. And using a regular bus route as a collection office was safer than it might appear. Crews changed shifts and routes. Passengers were just so much cargo to them, cargo to be picked up, given tickets, then unloaded again along the route.

'Eh . . . we're finished now?' queried the driver hopefully.

They weren't. From the bus, Thane took them over to the trees. Dan Laurence had rigged battery lamps and a canvas windbreak round the spot where Harry Freeman lay. Blue tape marked off the path to be used.

The Bureau men moved aside. Thane lifted one corner of the tarpaulin cover, exposed Freeman's face, and glanced at the bus crew.

Silently, the driver crossed himself. Beside him, the Pakistani nodded.

'He is the one, sair.'

'Go back to your bus,' Thane told them. 'But don't leave.'

They left and the Bureau team returned to work. One used what looked like a giant portable hair-dryer, blasting out a current of cold air strong enough to scatter the surface snow. Another moved in and carefully fanned the cleared area with an aerosol spray. A fine mist of red paint stained the white surface.

'Sorry about the colour,' grunted Laurence, appearing at Thane's elbow. 'But it gives us the best contrast on film negatives.' The Bureau chief grunted down on his knees, peered at the sprayed section, then rose. 'I'd say you're right. It was brushed over – but it's still interesting.'

'You've found something?'

'Aye.' Laurence, eyes narrowed, looked him over. 'But it'll keep till we're in the van. Anyway, Moss an' Doc Williams are in there, and we'll be damned lucky if they've left us as much as a sip of that coffee.'

Thane didn't argue.

Inside the van, a bottled-gas radiator glowed its heat to a cramped space surrounded by equipment racks, a laboratory bench and a tiny washbasin. As Laurence closed the door again, Moss and the police surgeon moved back from the radiator and let Thane take their place. For the first time he realized just how cold he felt.

'Half empty, damn them,' complained Laurence, examining his flask. 'Well, we deserve a bonus.' He poured coffee into two paper cups, opened a cupboard, and took out a bottle. A generous measure of tawny liquid splashed into each cup. 'Navy-issue rum, Colin – this'll heat your boots.' He handed one to Thane.

It burned its way down in an explosion of fire. Laurence took a long swallow at his own, hand-rolled a cigarette from an old pouch, stuck the result in his mouth, and lit it with a flaring of paper.

'Well, let's get on with it.' He stuck his hands deep into the sheepskin's pockets. 'First we've got car tracks. The blower and spray left them clear enough to work on. Give us some time and they'll talk a wee bit. Footprints beside the tyre tracks – better still. At least two men and certainly a woman. Footprints beside the body' – he picked a loose crumb of tobacco from his lips – 'ach, they made a good try at covering them up, but not good enough. A woman's high heels sink deeper into snow, compress down. She was

·100

there again, probably plus the others. Give us a wee bit time there too, and we should have something positive enough.'

As a start, it was better than Thane had hoped. He thanked Laurence with a nod, then turned to Doc Williams. 'Your side of it?'

The police surgeon sighed, rubbed his chin, and looked far from happy. 'You're not going to like this,' he warned.

'I don't like any of it,' said Thane wearily. 'Go on.'

'Quite simply I don't know what killed him,' said Williams slowly. 'There's no mark of violence visible. Phil says he had a cardiac condition. Correct?'

'He had, but he kept quiet about it.'

'Then a lot depends on the medical history.' Williams chose his words with care. 'If a man with a serious cardiac condition goes wandering around in what's near as dammit a blizzard, he's asking for trouble. He could drop dead – straightforward, natural cardiac failure.'

Thane stared at him. 'But with what we know –'

'My job is medical fact,' said the police surgeon doggedly. 'Right now medical fact is he has been dead for at least an hour, maybe more. In this kind of weather body temperature calculations are knocked to hell. But I can't say how or why he died. After a post mortem, yes. But not now.' He gave a rueful grimace. 'I'm sorry, Colin. But I told you already today life's low on miracles.'

'All right.' Thane's mouth tightened. 'First thing to get is his medical history. We'll contact the specialist who was treating him.'

'I tried,' said Moss, stirring in his corner. 'I phoned this Doctor Milne's office when Doc told me how things stood. We're out of luck. The receptionist was on her own, shutting up for the night. Milne's on his way out of town for a couple of days. Seems he has a flat in Glasgow, but his real home is up north at Glen Craig. He's on his way there now, driving. That's eighty miles, maybe three hours' travel on a night like this.'

'Then we'd better ask the Argyll County boys to help out,' mused Doc Williams. 'I need that information.'

Thane stayed silent for a moment, then shook his head. 'No. I'll go.'

'Drive up there, now?' Dan Laurence's snort of surprise knocked the ash from his cigarette. It dribbled a grey trail down his jacket. 'Haven't you got enough on your plate?'

'There's plenty to do,' agreed Thane wryly. 'But nothing's going to happen in a rush – not yet. Anyway, there's more than one reason why I want to talk to Milne.' He set down his cup and glanced at Moss. 'All right, Phil?'

'Aye.' Moss nodded his understanding. 'What do you want done with the bus crew?'

'Statements are enough for now. But we may need them again later.' He glanced at his watch. 'Doc, if you're finished here I'd appreciate a ride back to Millside. I'll collect my car there and go on.'

'Whenever you're ready.'

'Thanks. Phil, contact Milne's place at Glen Craig. Tell them I'm on my way, but better make it the full three hours before I'll arrive. There's something else I have to do first.'

Moss raised an eyebrow.

'Harry's wife,' said Thane quietly. 'Somebody has to tell her.'

Doc Williams picked up his medical bag and opened the van's door. The warm fog they'd built up vanished into the night.

Tuesday night in Glasgow is usually a quiet time in a cop's week. The part-time burglars and weekend rowdies have had their fill. Midweek league football, with its own trouble potential, is for Wednesday. Money is running low, but hasn't reached the empty-pockets stage of Thursday.

Most important of all, Tuesday's TV programmes are normally good enough to keep a fair slice of the population indoors.

By seven-thirty, when Phil Moss returned to Millside, only four new entries showed in the C.I.D. occurrence book. He glanced at them, decided they were minor, noted the men involved, then heard the telephone ringing in Thane's room. Grumbling to himself, he hurried through and scooped up the receiver.

'D.I. Moss –'

'At last,' barked Buddha Ilford's voice. Moss winced at the bellow and eased the phone away from his ear. The C.I.D. chief had a habit of relying on lung power when he telephoned. 'Where's Thane?'

'Out on inquiries, sir,' fenced Moss. 'The Harry Freeman business.'

'It may seem surprising, but I'd heard that much,' snapped Ilford. 'I still want to know where Thane is and what he's doing.'

Moss grimaced at the mouthpiece. 'He's on his way north to Glen Craig, sir. We've an important witness to contact – a doctor.'

'So a Divisional chief ups and offs – like that?' There was a long, pregnant silence.

'We need this doctor, sir,' defended Moss stubbornly.

'Maybe, but I've still to run what's supposed to be a detective force,' grated Ilford. 'I've asked Dan Laurence for a preliminary report from his side and I want a Divisional one. That'll have to be from you, Moss.' He ploughed straight on. 'Now, about this ned Cullen – if anyone at Millside still remembers him. Central Division have come up with something interesting. One of their pet informers says Cullen had a long session in a bar a few days back with another ned called Tank Lewis. Records say Lewis comes from Millside. Know him?'

'He's a regular customer.' Moss showed an immediate

103

spark of interest. 'Usually doubles as a driver and heavy – he was an army tank driver once, but they kicked him out.'

'I'm not interested in his medals,' said Ilford coldly. 'I'm thinking of the Alhambra warehouse job. Check him out, keep in touch, and don't forget that Freeman report.'

The receiver at the other end thumped down.

Moss shrugged, replaced his own receiver, and felt his ulcer kick. It looked like being a long night, he decided. Padding through to his own room, he opened the bottom drawer of the desk and ran a thoughtful eye over the waiting collection of bottles and pills. Moss settled for two tablespoons of olive oil, swallowed the stuff, lit a herbal cigarette to get rid of the taste, and sallied out again.

Two night-shift d.c.s on the tail of a meal break were his first victims. He dragged them from a half-hearted hand of cribbage and despatched them to check on Tank Lewis.

'But just check,' warned Moss. 'Don't bring him in.'

'That's getting to be the drill,' grinned one of the d.c.s. 'We just wait till they get killed off – it's easier.'

He drew a glare which made him wish he hadn't opened his mouth. But as the two men went out Moss had the same thought echoing in his mind. And there was still Sandy Lang. Nobody from Millside had as much as seen the bearded ex-confidence trickster so far. He didn't like it. Central Division could be relied on, but somehow he'd have been happier if the whole package was being handled under the one roof.

Moss belched, looked around, and spotted another night-shift man edging for the door. He called him back and spent the next ten minutes dictating a report for Ilford. It was detailed enough to keep the C.I.D. chief happy but vague enough to keep the basic options open.

The telephone in Thane's room rang again. Moss went through, answered, and heard Mary Thane's voice on the line.

'He's out, Mary,' he told her, relaxing. 'And he's liable to be pretty late getting back. We're having a rough day.'

'I thought you must when he didn't call.' There were sudden shouts in the background and he heard her tell the Thane children to take their noise somewhere else. 'Phil –'

'Still here,' he confirmed.

'Phil, has Colin told you about – well, what he's got on his mind just now?'

'No,' he confessed, leaning back against the desk. 'But I've guessed. He's going after some outside job, right?'

'An outside job is going after him,' she corrected. 'It's a good one, a bank security post. I – well, if he won't ask you, I'm going to do it. What do you think of the idea?'

Moss hesitated. 'For Colin? I don't know. It might work out. You'd like it, wouldn't you?'

'If *he* did. There didn't seem any doubt in it for me at first. But – now I'm not sure. He – he's –'

'Too much a cop?' Moss finished it for her. 'Mary, the one important thing is to let him do the deciding. But that won't be tonight. Harry Freeman's dead.'

'Oh no!' She was openly shocked. 'What happened?'

'We're not sure yet,' he said, more or less truthfully. 'But Colin's had to go out of town to talk to a doctor.'

She thanked him and said goodnight. Moss hung up, scratching his thinning hair. Well, he'd been right about Thane – but it was still none of his business, and there was plenty waiting which was.

He flicked the desk intercom switch for the duty orderly. 'Bring up Rab Hayes. And if there's any decent weak tea around I need it.'

The tea beat Hayes by a short head. Moss was leaning back in Thane's big chair, both hands wrapped round his cup, when the door opened. The money-lender came in warily with Detective Constable Beech as escort. Hayes wore a loud sports coat with a fawn roll-necked jersey and

105

slacks. The left side of his face was badly swollen and he looked anything but happy.

'I want a doctor or somethin',' mumbled Hayes from the unswollen side of his mouth. 'I'm in hell's own agony, Inspector.'

'Agony?' Moss raised a querulous eyebrow. 'Why?'

'It's like I said when you lifted me,' mumbled Hayes. 'I was at the dentist – got two teeth out. The fool must ha' done something wrong, and the pain's driving me crazy.' He straightened up a little. 'Anyway, you've no reason for keepin' me here. I've got rights.'

'People often say that at first,' mused Moss. 'But about this toothache – the prison dentist at Barlinnie is pretty good.' He glanced in straight-faced fashion at Beech. 'Think we could arrange something?'

'We could try there, sir,' agreed Beech solemnly. 'But Mr Hayes would need an appointment. The neds at Barlinnie keep breaking teeth. Too many files hidden in cakes.'

'What do you do for an encore?' snarled Hayes. 'Break into a soft-shoe routine?' He closed his mouth hard, yelped, and opened it quickly, clutching his jaw.

'You want to know why you're here?' Moss thumped down the tea cup and wished he hadn't as some of the contents slopped over Thane's 'In' tray. 'Harry Freeman is dead.'

'The bookie?' Hayes shrugged uneasily. 'What's it got to do with me?'

'Everything,' said Moss softly. 'He was helping us. And when you warned The Tallyman that Chief Inspector Thane was digging again you put the finger straight on to Freeman.'

It got home. Hayes whitened but still shook his head. 'Not me. I didn't warn anybody.'

'It couldn't be anyone else.' Moss kept his tone at the same quiet, iron-hard level. 'Beech –'

'Sir?'

'Go outside, shut the door, and stay outside.'

Beech went out. As the door closed again, Moss got up and walked round until he stood in front of the man. He eyed Hayes with open contempt.

The money-lender swallowed hard. 'What's going on?'

'I'll tell you,' said Moss, spacing out each word. 'Hayes, I'm tired. I've an ulcer. You think your mouth is giving you hell? Then my ulcer is doing double that. So I'm impatient.' One thin, bony hand took hold of the sports coat by the lapels. He tugged gently. 'Hayes, I'm impatient and I don't like you. I haven't eaten since I had lunch. And we're all alone.'

Hayes tried to draw back. 'You can't threaten me –'

'Threaten you?' Moss tightened his grip on the cloth. 'I'm asking a question. Who did you contact?'

'I didn't –'

Deliberately, Moss lowered his right heel on to the toe of the man's left shoe and left it there.

'Try again.'

'You – you don't understand.' It came like a wail from the puffy mouth. Hayes's eyes began to water.

'Try me,' suggested Moss.

'If – if I hadn't tipped them off about Thane they'd have found out sooner or later. Then they'd have come after me for not telling them. Inspector, you – you know that!'

'You're doing better, much better.' Moss moved his heel clear but kept his grip of the cloth. 'Who's The Tallyman?'

'I don't know. I mean it.' The words came as fast as his swollen jaw would allow and with a desperation which meant truth. 'My contact is a woman. She – she came to me a few months back. Strictly a business proposition, it was. If I let them know names of people turned down for loans they'd pay me.' He glanced away, seeking some kind of justification. 'Maybe – maybe you could call it just an introductory commission.'

'I'd call it something else.' Releasing him, Moss looked

at his hand with something close to disgust and rubbed it on the desk. 'Tell me about the woman.'

'I contact her at a phone number. Her name is Janey Milton.'

The name meant nothing on its own. But a woman fitted only too well with what had happened to Freeman. Moss grunted. 'Janey Milton – the original Paradise Lost?'

Hayes blinked, baffled. 'If you mean looks, she's not bad. She's blonde, probably around thirty.'

'That's all you know?' Moss waited a moment and was satisfied. He raised his voice. 'Beech – come and take this animal away.'

Hayes was led off. Beech would take his statement and run a check on Janey Milton and her telephone number.

Glad it was over, Moss leaned back against the desk and wondered what he'd have done if Rab Hayes had called his bluff. But then they seldom did. Meet fear with fear, and the more immediate of the two usually won the day.

It was a dirty way. It left a taste in his mouth. But as long as it worked he'd leave the moralizing to someone else.

He straightened up as the duty orderly entered with a teleprinter flimsy. Moss glanced at it, then read it again with more interest. The other figure still in their background detail was on the move again, but this time with apparent purpose. The Central men shadowing Sandy Lang reported their quarry had taken a bus from town but left it again after a couple of fare stages and was now on his way back in. He'd spoken to no one. As a journey, it had all the appearance of a precautionary shake-off.

Moss sensed the temptation, liked it, and made up his mind.

'I'm going out,' he told the orderly. 'If Headquarters start making a noise about where I am, just say something turned up.'

*   *   *

108

Fifteen minutes and a scatter of radio messages later, Phil Moss left the duty car at the corner of Gordon Street and Buchanan Street, close to the heart of the city. The snow had stopped and plenty of late-night theatregoers were splashing a cheerful way through the slush. A girl smiled from a closed but brightly lit shop doorway. She looked about twenty-five, which probably meant she was seventeen. The smile was for a boy hurrying towards her.

He kept on. Another figure stepped from a darker doorway. The Central man, a fair-haired d.c. with a small moustache, nodded a greeting, then murmured quietly into the tiny two-way radio he held in one hand. It was the pocket-size unit more usually used by beat patrolmen in outlying areas. The speaker unit murmured back and he was satisfied.

'Lang's where I left him, sir. My mate's watching – there's a lane we can use.'

Moss followed him. The lane was dark and empty and led into a courtyard, then another lane. At the far end, the second Central man was waiting and waved them on. Moss found himself looking out into the business section of Harald Street, almost empty, with only the street lights burning.

'Over there, sir,' murmured the watcher. 'That doorway on the left, across the road. I can't make out what he's doing, but he's been there some time now.'

Moss peered across, saw a tall, thin figure leaning casually against the doorway, and waited. Suddenly the figure moved, turned his back on them for a moment, then swung round again.

'He's done that a few times,' said the Central man, puzzled.

'If it was anywhere else, I'd say he was trying to break into the place on his own.'

'You're sure he's Lang – and there's no one else?'

Both men nodded.

'Well, he doesn't know me.' Moss stuck a cigarette into his mouth, left it unlit, winked at them, and wandered casually out of the lane. He crossed Harald Street at a right angle, turned as he reached the opposite pavement, and trudged along through the slush, hands deep in his coat pockets. He sensed as much as saw Lang watching him approach the doorway.

'Hey.' Moss stopped and grinned hopefully. 'Got a light, friend?'

The bearded face frowned and then nodded. Moss came nearer while Lang searched his pockets and produced a box of matches.

'Ta.' As the man struck a match Moss bent over the flame, cupping his hands to shield it, just touching the man's fingers. They were quivering a little.

'Thanks again.' He stepped back, drew on the cigarette, and headed on up the street.

As he went, he fought down an urge to chuckle.

There had been a clink of metal when Lang found those matches. Colin Thane would have been interested, particularly interested – if he'd known that one of The Tallyman's bunch was paying such close attention to the Bank of Central Scotland's front door!

From the city, the route to Glen Craig began with the winding snake of a road along the side of Loch Lomond. It meant a skidding, slithering fight to make time, and Colin Thane knew relief when that part was behind and the Austin began climbing into the high country.

Something else lay behind him – the memory of Lil Freeman's face, the half hour he'd spent with her until friendly neighbours had taken over.

The car wallowed through an unexpected drift and he swore. He'd had time now to think. In a strange way, the combined physical and mental effort involved in keeping the car from floundering into the nearest snow-filled ditch left the rest of his mind free and clear.

He'd gone right back to the night at the Lombok Club when he'd talked to Harry. Nobody, not even Phil Moss, had known he was going to try to contact the bookmaker. And Herb Cullen had been there before he arrived, his task obviously Jim Manneson, his attention on the young bank clerk's efforts at the roulette wheel.

Then the tip-off that Millside Division had a sudden new interest in The Tallyman. If Cullen's orders to 'warn off' Harry Freeman had come before he left the club . . .

No, it was unlikely. But had Josh Barbar been at the Lombok that night by chance? Or had he also been there to watch the bank clerk and learned more than he'd expected? Was it Barbar at the top, Barbar who was 'milking' his own agency files?

The Argyll County boundary sign glinted in the head-lamps as he formed the inevitable conclusion. If Josh Barbar, debt collector, would-be security agent, was the reality behind the shadowy figure of The Tallyman, then a whole lot of things made sense.

Mind still working round it, Thane automatically checked the time. Two hours had passed since he'd left the city, which represented fairly fast travel. But it was still a journey through an empty, white alien world, his car apparently alone on the road. Though the blizzard had died and the Argyll snowplough teams had obviously been busy, a strong wind was trying hard to reclaim what the big plough blades had won back. The outside temperature was still falling. He caught glimpses of mountain burns, frozen solid in the very act of tumbling over rocks.

Glen Craig was on the edge of that year-round desolation called the Rannoch Moor. Thane swung left at the road sign and the car fought along a narrower way, a twisting track which would have been bad enough in daylight.

At last he saw the lights of a house ahead and knew he'd arrived. He turned off on to a short length of private driveway and finally stopped outside a tall, neo-Gothic mansion which might have been lifted straight out of a Victorian etching. Built of dark stone, it even had a miniature roof turret to one side.

Thane got out, treated himself to the luxury of an animal-like stretch, and noticed another car parked a little distance away. It was a silver-grey Alfa Romeo coupé, the grille festooned with badges and extra spotlamps. Curious, he crossed over and felt heat still coming from its radiator grille.

The wind whipped his clothes. He shivered, and hurried towards the house. An old-fashioned brass bell-pull hung to one side of the front door and he yanked it hard.

A few moments passed. He was reaching for the bell-pull again when the heavy wooden door suddenly swung open.

Thane got ready to speak. Then the words died. The man framed in the hall light was Josh Barbar.

Barbar looked at him, brushed back his long, coppery hair with one hand, and grinned.

'Come on in, Thane,' he invited. 'We wondered if you'd make it.'

Chapter Six

Wordlessly, Colin Thane entered a long, broad, old-fashioned hallway. A log fire burned in a great iron fireplace halfway down, the flames dancing on polished wood and glinting on decorative horse brasses which hung along the walls.

'Surprised to see me?' asked Josh Barbar briskly, closing the door behind them.

'You're a few miles from home,' said Thane neutrally, glancing around. 'And those roads are no picnic – when did you get here?'

'Just before your people phoned to say you were coming,' said Barbar easily. 'Helen invited me – Doctor Milne's daughter. You met her at the Lombok.' Thane nodded, and Barbar chuckled. 'To be honest, I volunteered to bring her up. She wasn't quite sure when her father would make it.

'Still, he's here now. Leave your coat and I'll take you through. I'm acting butler – this is the housekeeper's night off.'

Thane peeled off coat and hat, hung them on one of a row of pegs, and turned to the sparkling fire for a moment. Warming his hands, face expressionless, he asked, 'You know why I've come?'

'I read the note the housekeeper left,' said Barbar. 'Pity about Harry Freeman – I know he was a friend of yours. But I suppose when you've a bad heart you never know the moment.' He gave a slight shrug. 'That's what I can't understand. Couldn't you have done all this by phone? I mean – well, it's just one of those things, isn't it?'

'Like you said, he was a friend.' Thane turned from the fire, meeting the pale eyes glinting behind those rimless glasses. 'Harry died in the open, alone. That could mean an inquiry, delays – and his wife has enough sorrow on her plate. If Doctor Milne certifies the medical background I can cut some of the red tape.'

It was a lie in fact and substance, but it was near to what might happen in some cases – and the best he could dredge up at such shattering short notice. Barbar considered things for a moment and seemed satisfied.

'So when anyone's time comes things are a lot easier if they're respectably in bed,' paraphrased Barbar. 'Well, it's hard luck all round.' Still talking, he led the way down the hall and opened a door.

They went into a big, comfortably furnished room with heavy, gilt-framed oil paintings on the walls. An even larger log fire threw out its heat and Helen Milne sat on a rug to one side of the hearth, hands clasped round her knees. The girl's raven hair contrasted with a white wool sweater and a tight red cat-suit, and she smiled a greeting as the man in a chair near her got to his feet.

'You've come a long way, Chief Inspector, and on a devil of a night.' Doctor Norman Milne was off duty and looked the part in a baggy russet tweed suit with leather patches at the elbows and cuffs. A white-haired, hawk-faced man in his late fifties, his handclasp was hard and firm, the manner quietly assured.

'It's late to come calling,' apologized Thane. 'But I'd no option.'

'Don't worry about it. Get in front of that fire and thaw out. You'll have a dram.' The heart specialist made it more statement than invitation and nodded to his daughter.

114

'Pour the man a whisky, girl – and don't drown it in water like you usually do.'

Helen Milne chuckled, uncurled, and got to her feet. 'Ice, Mr Thane?'

'And that's a heathen thought on a night like this,' declared her father. He glanced at Thane for approval as the girl crossed to their liquor cabinet, then went on. 'Sorry you missed me in town – and I'm even more sorry about Freeman. He was one of my favourite patients.'

'The Chief Inspector says he wants you to help him through some formalities about the death,' volunteered Barbar flopping into a chair. 'This red-tape business seems crazy to me. What difference does it make where Freeman died when it was an obvious heart attack?'

'Aye.' Milne sucked his teeth and glanced at Thane as the girl returned with a well-filled glass. 'Well, there's form-filling in death as much as life. I'll be happy to do the usual.'

Thane took the whisky, raised his glass in a perfunctory, silent toast to his host, and sipped the liquor. 'I hoped you'd say that,' he told Milne, his face impassive. 'It shouldn't take too long.'

'And I'll leave you to it,' declared Barbar unexpectedly, glancing at his watch. 'Ten o'clock – I won't make the city till after midnight. If those roads get any worse' – he grimaced – 'Helen was worried enough on the way up, and it will be worse now.'

'If your driving was its usual standard I'd have got out and walked,' said Doctor Milne, frowning. 'Look, stay the night if you want – the spare room's always ready.'

Quickly, Barbar shook his head. 'No thanks. I've too much work first thing tomorrow if I'm going to manage that time off to come deer-bashing with you and Helen.'

'The term is "stalking",' growled Milne with limited humour. 'And with any luck, some damned stag will get you in the process, though I think I'd prefer his head on my wall to yours.'

'Josh would make a pretty poor hatstand,' said Helen Milne with a gurgling laugh. 'His ears aren't big enough, for a start.'

Barbar brushed a long strand of hair back from his forehead and smiled lazily. 'Don't expect me to apologize for that. But maybe Thane could use your father's offer – he's had a long day.'

'People will be waiting for me back in Glasgow,' said Thane, crisply forestalling the invitation. 'When does the shooting party get under way, Doctor?'

'First thing Thursday morning,' said Milne. 'We've a reasonable stretch of deer forest fairly near. It's closed season for stags, but the landowner is keen to thin down his hind population.' Hands in his pockets, he turned to Barbar. 'Josh, I'll leave Helen to see you on your way – what time will you be back tomorrow?'

'Evening sometime.'

'Good. Chief Inspector, we'll go through to my study. Bring your glass.'

They left Barbar and the girl, went through the hall, and entered a small, book-lined room which smelled strongly of leather. A gun rack held a selection of rifles and shotguns.

Milne closed the door, switched on an electric radiator, then crossed to a desk near the curtained window and flipped open a box of cigarettes. 'You've a family, Thane?'

'Yes, but still school age.' Thane took one of the offered cigarettes and accepted a light.

'Then you've plenty still ahead of you.' Milne sat down, waving him into another chair.

Outside, from the hall, Thane heard Barbar's voice. The girl answered, laughing. The outer door opened, slammed shut after a few moments, and the next sound was the bark of the Alfa's engine and the throb of its exhaust as it got under way.

Milne sighed. 'I'm a widower. Have been for a few years. Teen-age daughters are bad enough, but later – damned if I know where Helen dredges up some of her friends, and the best policy is to say nothing. Go along with them.' His mouth closed briefly and he leaned back. 'I went along with you back there, Thane. What's this nonsense about driving up just to get a medical certificate?'

'It made a reasonable excuse.' Thane sipped his glass.

'But a poor one.' The heart specialist grunted to himself. 'All right, let's not waste time. What do you want? An outline of Freeman's medical condition?'

'For a start, yes.'

'The thing is straightforward enough.' Milne rubbed a finger absently along his nose. 'Harry Freeman suffered from a fairly common cardiac condition, and he first came to me about a year ago, after he suffered what a layman would call a minor heart attack. I examined him, there were traces of degenerative cardiovascular lesions, and I had him electrocardiographed. There were positive traces of myocardial degenerative changes – degenerative changes of the heart muscle. I began prescribing drug therapy and told him he'd have to lead a more placid life.'

'I see.' Thane probed on, uncertain. 'How serious was his condition?'

'Provided he behaved himself, followed my rules and avoided major emotional strain, he'd no need to worry.' Milne put his head to one side, eyeing Thane expectantly. 'Now, supposing you tell me what happened? You came here for a reason – and if I can respect a patient's confidences I can respect yours.'

Thane sipped his drink again, then nodded. 'Harry Freeman was helping me with – well, inquiries. I'd told

117

him he'd done enough, but he kept on. When he left your surgery this afternoon he took a bus trip. I think the result was he met certain people – dangerous people.' He shrugged a little. 'When we found Harry he was lying in the open, among trees, and he'd been dead over an hour. The police surgeon says there's no outward sign of physical violence.'

'Yet you still wonder how he died?' There was something approaching despair in Milne's voice. 'Freeman was already in a state of tension when I saw him this afternoon. His blood pressure was up several points.' One hand slapped flat on the desk. 'Man, it's simple enough. I've patients whose lives are in the hands of any fool who cares to upset them.' He gave a long sigh which ended in a scowl. 'Emotional strain, physical strain, this abominable weather, all those things would weigh against Freeman. Even though I –' He stopped short and shook his head. 'No, you can't work those things out like a mathematical table.'

But there had been hesitation, and Thane seized on it. 'Yet you're surprised, Doctor?'

'I didn't say that,' corrected Milne sharply. 'I might have thought it fairly unlikely he'd go like that, but there's no reason why it couldn't happen. Anyway, the post-mortem report will take care of things. You've come a long way for very little.' The thought triggered another and his manner changed. 'When did you eat last?'

'A good while back, but –'

'Then I'm a damned poor host. I won't be long.' Milne sprang to his feet and went out of the room in purposeful fashion.

Wearily, Thane settled back in his chair. If nothing else, he at least understood now Harry Freeman's sudden fresh interest in helping to nail The Tallyman. The story of the unknown heart patient who'd been hounded to death had struck home and struck hard in a way oddly typical of

Freeman's reactions. Struck hard – and in turn had helped kill him.

Doctor Milne was gone roughly five minutes. When footsteps returned, it was his daughter who entered first carrying a tray with sandwiches and coffee. She laid it on the desk.

'Help yourself,' invited Milne, coming in behind her. 'Helen was making it anyway – I just speeded the service a little.' Eyes twinkling, he tapped his daughter lightly on the shoulder. 'And now I've a chance, maybe you'll tell me why you came up tonight instead of staying at the flat till tomorrow, like we'd planned.'

'Josh phoned me and suggested it. He likes driving on snow,' she told him cheerfully. 'It seemed a good idea; you were going to be on your own, remember?'

Milne looked pleased but still frowned a little. 'I could have brought you myself, if you'd asked.'

She sighed and turned to Thane. 'Fathers can be a problem, Chief Inspector. I'm afraid mine doesn't approve of my taste in things – like Josh, for instance.'

'Everyone has problems,' said Thane dryly. Then, with what he hoped sounded like friendly curiosity, he asked, 'When did he call you? I met him this morning and he didn't mention it.'

'Not till this afternoon, just after two o'clock. I'd just got back to the flat from a job.'

'And when did you leave Glasgow?' Quickly, he explained, 'I'm interested in just how fast people can make this journey.'

'Well' – she thought for a moment – 'Josh picked me up at the flat around five-thirty and we got here just after seven-thirty. Not much more than the two hours.'

'Too damned quickly in this weather,' declared Milne soberly.

'That's what I told him.' Unconcerned, she winked at her father and left them.

Milne poured coffee into the two cups and nodded his approval as Thane helped himself. 'Now, where were we?' he asked.

'At the stage where Harry Freeman's death was just one of those things.' Thane spoke through a mouthful of sandwich. The filling was lean, tender venison.

'But you're not satisfied?'

'I want to make sure,' said Thane quietly. 'I want to be very sure, Doctor. Because I know the kind of people he came up against.' He put down the sandwich. 'Would you ever discuss a patient's condition with anyone other than a medical colleague?'

'No.' Milne's eyes narrowed. 'It would be damned unethical. Why?'

'Harry told nobody he had heart trouble,' said Thane, the words coming slowly. 'Even his wife found out by accident. Yet if someone knew, if someone decided to play on it –'

Milne's mouth twisted angrily. 'I don't like what you're trying to suggest.'

'I'm suggesting what I've got to find out, Doctor. If I stand on anyone's toes, that's incidental.' He rose and crossed over to the gun rack, touching the cold metal of the nearest rifle. It was a Winchester .270, Milne's initials carved into the walnut stock. 'You can kill a man a lot of ways. A bullet is simple. But if someone wanted to fake natural death, that would take a degree of acquired knowledge. Wouldn't it?'

The heart specialist had been listening with gathering impatience. But suddenly the impatience died and his expression faded into a near resemblance of caution. A long moment passed, then he gave a reluctant, fractional nod.

'And there might be a way, Doctor?'

Milne settled again behind his desk. He reached care-

120

fully for another cigarette and lit it. 'Are you working around to saying the knowledge had to come from me?'

'Yes – but given innocently.'

'That's something, I suppose.' Milne sighed and ran a hand unhappily across his forehead. 'When you arrived here you told a story which – well, you knew I wouldn't accept. Will you tell me the real reason for doing it?'

Silently, Thane shook his head.

'Thane, I' – Milne moistened his thin lips – 'I'm very proud of my daughter.'

'What I've seen of her I like,' said Thane softly. He came round opposite the man, leaning his hands on the desk. 'But daughters can pose problems when they meet – strangers.'

Suddenly, Milne stubbed out the cigarette with a savage violence. 'How do I contact your police surgeon?'

'If you telephone Police Headquarters in Glasgow they'll locate him.' Thane paused hopefully. 'You've something in mind?'

'Now, yes.' The reluctance had gone. In its place was a weary bitterness from a man who seemed to have aged, yet a man who spoke with a new, coldly professional detachment. 'Something anyone in the cardiac trade knows about, even if he usually ignores it. Ever heard of vagal inhibition?'

'No, but I'd like to.'

'There's a little story which explains it best,' said Milne softly, leaning forward, his white hair glinting in the light, fingertips together on the desk. 'Not quite two hundred years ago a man Downie was janitor at Aberdeen University. He was a sneak, a nark – or so the story goes. He plagued the students, until they decided to teach him a lesson. They seized him, held a mock trial, and condemned him to death.'

'Nice people, students,' murmured Thane.

'Quite.' Milne managed a suspicion of a smile. 'Downie

121

was blindfolded and dragged to an "execution block" – and by then he was in a state of terror. They bared his neck and forced his head down on the block. He was told to make peace with his Maker – and a student flicked him on the back of the neck with a wet towel.

'They meant to scare him. Instead, he died. Vagal inhibition – shock to one of the main signal centres of the nervous system while the subject was in a state of emotional anxiety.' Milne drew his fingers tight together. 'The vagus nerves extend to the heart. When they – well, seize up if you like because of shock, the heart can stop. The man dies. Especially a man in Harry Freeman's condition.'

'But' – Colin Thane gnawed his lip, struggling to grasp the inference – 'but it would show in a post mortem?'

'Depends how it was done. It might with some methods – if you knew exactly what you were looking for. If you didn't' – Milne shook his head – 'only that there'd been cardiac inhibition, plain, ordinary heart failure. But vagal inhibition happens in different ways. It might happen to an athlete if he finished a long run on a hot day, then gulped a drink of ice water. Shock, Thane – a different kind of shock, with the same result. Or if a man had a full meal and then was –' He stopped and shrugged. 'There are plenty of ways. Let's concentrate on Freeman. He was dressed for outdoors?'

'Yes.' Thane stepped back from the desk and sat down, waiting.

'I can rule out a few things,' mused Milne. 'Look, I'll need time to think – but I promise I'll telephone your police surgeon tonight.'

'I'd appreciate it.' Thane knew he had to go on. 'Doctor, I need to know the rest. Did you discuss Freeman's death with anyone before I arrived?'

'With Barbar, you mean?' Milne's mouth tightened. 'Stop talking like a comic-book detective. Put a label on him.'

'All right, did you talk about it with Barbar?'

'No.' Milne shook his head firmly. 'But Freeman's name was on the telephone message and I'm a heart man. Any fool could put two and two together.'

'Could Barbar know about Freeman's condition before tonight – find out about it any way from you?'

'It's possible,' admitted Milne slowly. 'He might have seen Freeman at my surgery sometime if he was meeting Helen there. Or – well, maybe Helen told him. She knows who most of my patients are.'

Thane reached for his coffee cup, found it had gone cold, and laid it aside. 'And there's a reason why Barbar would know about vagal inhibition?'

'I must be making it pretty obvious.' The older man grimaced unhappily. 'I made a joke about it a few weeks back, while I was complaining about Helen dumping ice in my drink. Barbar was interested.'

'So you told him how it could be done – in detail?'

'In fine detail. The expert showing off his knowledge.' The words grated out. 'What happens now?'

'We work on it, like we're working on some other things,' Thane told him. 'But there's another way you can help. Say nothing to your daughter. And act normally when Barbar arrives tomorrow.'

'Normally is one stage short of open dislike,' said Milne wearily. 'I'll manage.'

Thane smiled and got to his feet. 'Then I'll get on my way.'

Milne came with him out into the hall, helped him on with his coat, then insisted on coming out to the Austin to see him off.

Outside, the sky had cleared, stars sparkled like diamonds, and the snow was ice-crisp underfoot. The wind had dropped a little and a fox was barking somewhere in the distance.

'Good weather for stalking.' Milne drew himself more

123

erect, looking around. 'The snow brings the herds down from the high glens.' He glanced at Thane's shadowy figure. 'A modern rifle kills from a long distance, Chief Inspector. But up here we believe in getting in close, making very sure before a trigger is pulled. That's – well, the sporting way.'

Thane nodded his understanding. 'There's no sport in my job, Doctor – though there can be a devil of a lot of gamesmanship. But I know what you mean. And we'll be in very close – through necessity.'

At least he now had most of the questions. Tomorrow should bring more of the answers. Tiredness evaporated, Thane felt a new confidence as he drove back from Glen Craig towards the A82 trunk junction.

The snow lay tight-packed, smoothed by the wind, the ice-crisp surface treacherous on the bends, but he built up to a steady pace. Part of his mind began planning, dividing out the next stages into those the Millside Division team could accomplish and the items which would need Headquarters help. A long ribbon of straight appeared in the headlights, and Thane increased speed until the Austin was shading just below forty-five. With luck, he should be back in the city before two a.m.

The straight ended and he eased the accelerator as his lights showed another bend ahead, tight and sharp, curling round a shoulder of raw rock on the right, brinking on a downward slope to the left.

Speedometer still dropping, the car swung smoothly into the corner. He began whistling softly, the tune an old bagpipe lament.

The lament suddenly choked. Velvet night became an eye-stabbing dazzle of white as a glare of headlamps flared to light, flared as someone palmed switches simultaneously and at least six powerful lamps pinned the Austin in their concentrated brilliance.

Blinded, he jabbed instinctively for the brake pedal. The Austin's rear wheels broke loose and the car began a mad, skidding lurch.

Solid rock or the downward slope. The slope offered more chance but the car was sliding for the rock.

Rear-wheel skids should be steered into, said the rule-books. But that took for granted a wide road, not a narrow track, took for granted that you weren't skating for imminent disaster at head-on speed.

His mind began working in the rule-breaking, reflex training hammered home by a laconic Traffic sergeant who'd once ruled the Headquarters driving course.

Right foot clear of the accelerator. Swing the wheel hard left, against the skid. Let the skid switch into a spin, wait that fraction of a second. With near computer accuracy Thane declutched, wrenched on the hand brake to lock the rear wheels, then released it again.

The spin became a complete sideways skid, all four tyres scrabbling, treads moaning as they scraped in the most powerful slowing force any car can exert.

He was heading away from the rock, still pinned in that glare, still working blind, knowing the inevitable. The car reached the edge of the slope and, still travelling sideways, seemed to hesitate before it swayed on its springs and gently rolled.

The world spun. Loose tools clattered at the rear and he was thrown from behind the wheel. There was a thud as the car jolted on its wheels again. It swayed into another roll, then halted in a crash of metal and a shattering of glass.

The car had come to rest, half on its side but right way up. The engine had stalled, and Thane realized that other frantic, rasping noise was his own breathing. He'd been shoved halfway under the scuttle, one foot was tangled with the pedals, and he'd caught a thump on the head.

Up above, the glare of light on snow died to a faint glow.

An engine fired and was followed by the rasping bellow of a powerful exhaust. He listened, tensed, as the car turned on the road. Then it went growling off, gathering speed, heading for the trunk junction.

Still dazed, Thane freed his coat, struggled to open a door and thankfully half-clambered half-fell out into a bank of snow.

The Austin had rolled almost forty feet, then jammed against a gnarled, stunted tree, stoving in its body just behind the front wheels. A thick branch had smashed one of the side windows, and another branch, snapped, disappeared somewhere beneath the engine area.

He struggled upright and made a wry inspection of the rest. Like some soft cushion, the snow had saved him – and maybe the car. Despite that roll, the roof wasn't marked. But at best it would be a long time before the Austin could be driven again.

Thane turned his back on the tree and floundered up the slope to the roadway. A little way along, close against the rock, he found the spot where the other car had waited. Tyre marks were there, beginning to fill in the keening wind. A tiny blotch of sump oil lay between them.

The battery of lights and sports-car exhaust, a driver who could choose his spot so carefully – it spelled out Josh Barbar in plain enough terms.

But why do it, then drive off without checking? Unless Barbar hadn't cared very much about a choice between killing or merely injuring, was concerned only with making sure of time, time without risk.

Time for a reason.

Thane shivered and not completely because of the cold. He reckoned he was still a couple of miles short of the A82, pulled up his coat collar, and began walking.

It was past midnight when he reached the junction. After ten minutes a newspaper truck came along, stopped and picked him up. He got a lift from there to the nearest

126

village, found the tiny police station, and started using its telephone.

An Argyll County car finally deposited Thane outside his home at three a.m. He watched it drive off, then went in as quietly as he could.

The dog growled once from the kitchen, then settled. A note was propped against the telephone, in Mary's writing.

'Phil called. Headquarters conference without fail at eight a.m. He wants to see you first. The alarm's set for six. Love.'

Three hours' sleep, he decided, was probably better than none.

A tall, age-blackened building in St. Andrew Street, flanked by tenements, a working men's hostel and some old warehouses, Glasgow's Police Headquarters is always at its lowest ebb before dawn on a winter's morning.

The calendar said Wednesday. The morning paper headlines forecast another rise in income tax. The first of the day clerical staff crept into the brightly lit beehive of corridors, faces still struggling to appear awake. Trudging around, the uniformed staff waited for the first scent of sausages grilling in the ground-floor canteen, the signal for coffee-and-rolls salvation.

Shaved and breakfasted, Thane arrived with Phil Moss in the duty car exactly on the stroke of eight a.m. Behind them lay a rushed discussion at Millside, and ahead, they knew, lay a possible scalding session.

Pushing in through the glass entrance doors, Thane caught a glimpse of his tired-eyed reflection and groaned aloud.

Moss gave a dry grunt of amusement. 'They work better hours at that bank, Colin. Made up your mind yet?'

'Eh?' Halfway through the doors, Thane stopped in his tracks. 'Who the devil told you about –' he broke off as two

127

uniformed branch sergeants pushed past, then more or less dragged his wiry second-in-command into the main hallway. As the doors slammed shut behind them, he demanded again, 'Who told you?'

'I pretty well guessed, seeing you doing the tip-toe act yesterday,' said Moss sardonically. 'But I got the details from Mary. She thought you were going to tell me about it anyway.'

'Well, I – I meant to, sooner or later.' Thane felt awkwardly on the defensive, without being sure why. And all he'd seen of Mary that morning had been over a five-minute breakfast, most of that taken up explaining about the car and answering questions about his interview for the bank job. 'What about it, Phil? Wouldn't you take it?'

'Me?' Sadly, Moss shook his head. 'I can't look after my own money, let alone other people's. But it sounds a nice cosy billet – if you don't need the old excitements.'

'Excitements? Like wrecking my car and wondering if Special Purposes Fund will pay the repair bill?' He drew a deep breath. 'I've a final interview at their head office tomorrow. After that, I think I'll be buying a nice, rolled umbrella.'

'You?' Moss jeered at the notion. 'Give you an umbrella and you'd look like a performing bear!'

'Better that than a – a –' Thane's irate growl died as the main doors slammed again and Buddha Ilford came towards them, his moonface red with cold.

''Morning,' grated the C.I.D. chief, the courtesy a strained effort. He thumbed towards the waiting elevator. 'Well, let's get on with it. I've booked the conference room.'

They followed meekly, though the trip was only one floor up. When Chief Superintendent William Ilford was in his early-morning mood it was best to tag along quietly.

The conference room, long and narrow, held a simple

central table, chairs, and a sideboard proudly filled with silver cups won by the Headquarters golf team – though any of the divisions would complain the Headquarters mob had more time to practise than most. And it already had two occupants when they entered. Dan Laurence slouched low in a chair, thumbs in his waistcoat, a cigarette threatening to singe his lip. He looked tired. So did Doc Williams, whose usually crisp shirt collar was limp and sweat-stained. They caught the police surgeon in the act of washing down a pill with a glass of water.

'Vitamin B,' he explained greyly after the perfunctory greetings. 'No good to you, Phil. But they help with hangovers, fatigue, or downright misery – and I've got the lot.'

They settled quickly round the table, Buddha Ilford at its head, Thane and Moss on one side, Laurence and Williams wary allies on the other. Ilford took time for the ritual of getting his briar pipe going, then cleared his throat with a hoarse rasp.

'We know why we're here and you've all had copies of Thane's telephoned report of what happened when he went north. Correct?' They nodded, he sucked at his pipe, then glanced at Thane. 'How's the car?'

'Being towed in today sometime,' said Thane glumly. 'It could be a write-off.'

'Unfortunate,' said Ilford with minimum sympathy. 'Anyway, I called this meeting early for obvious reasons. There are matters which may require action before the Central Scotland head office opens for today. We'll take it for granted this ned Lang wasn't trying the bank door for amusement and this damned clerk –ah –'

'Manneson,' prompted Moss.

Ilford threw him a glare. 'I was going to say this damned clerk is almost certainly their inside man, buying his way off The Tallyman's hook.' He sighed and shook his head. 'I'd like to know more about the security arrangements inside that place, but the Central Scotland is like most banks – too damned confident in its own ability.'

'Sir' – unabashed, Moss interrupted again – 'Chief Inspector Thane has some details.'

'Well, Thane?'

'They're pretty good, sir.' Below the table Thane clenched a fist as he mentally consigned Phil Moss to the nearest inferno. 'The strong-room would be impossible on a safe-blowing approach, there's an interacting locking system which couldn't be broken without several executives getting into the act, and I can't see a straight bandit-type daylight raid – not unless they used an army.'

'Yet they've something brewing.' Ilford locked his jaws around the pipe's stem, frowning.

'We'd better give the bank some kind of a hint,' rumbled Laurence, removing the last fragment of cigarette from his lips and stubbing it.

'Thane?' Ilford raised a questioning eyebrow.

Colin Thane had a brief, inward struggle between his present and future, but finally shook his head. 'I wouldn't – or I'd leave it as late as possible, sir. The top brass over there would automatically start tightening up, and The Tallyman's bunch would probably know within the hour.' His mouth tightened. 'I want to nail this bunch in the act, get them for the maximum, with no chance of them wriggling clear.'

At his side, Phil Moss gave a cautious belch of disagreement. 'You're forgetting we're hoping to land some of them on a murder charge,' he reminded. Then, more pointedly, for Thane's benefit, he added, 'And if the bank bosses find out we used them as bait they'll kick up hell. The way they'll see it, we left them at risk – and banks don't like risks.'

'You're both right,' mused Ilford. 'But I go along with Thane on one thing. Even if we're lucky, we won't get them all on a murder count. And I want this organization pulverized, once and for all.'

'I'm just a humble medical man,' said Doc Williams easily. 'But couldn't you squeeze this bank clerk a little?'

'I've got that in mind,' agreed Thane grimly. He leaned forward, his eyes on Ilford. 'Last night I was told to put a label on things. Let's do it. Josh Barbar will be at that bank this morning. He's also going to keep some sort of a watch on young Manneson. But Phil and I could talk to Manneson's wife this morning – and Manneson always comes home for lunch. We'd still be there.'

'Which means a gamble on making him see sense.' Ilford went into a pipe-sucking contemplation, then nodded. 'Do that. Now, let's turn to things we're sure about. I – ah – relieved Millside of one chore last night. I went to Barlinnie Prison and saw Andrew Fergan.' A faint smile flickered across his face. 'It seemed no harm to hint at the possibility of a fairly early parole and he was willing enough to cooperate. Fergan had dealings with the Barbar debt-collection people. Then, about a month later, he had a money offer from The Tallyman – same pattern as the others and, like the majority, no "buying out" offer involved.'

'You've got to admit it is neat,' murmured Dan Laurence. 'You use ex-cops to run a legitimate business – then milk their information. Crafty.' He shifted heavily in his chair. 'Well, thanks to the benefits of superior education an' despite the fact we're crammed up in a cluster of flaming attic rooms, I can say the Scientific Bureau triumphs again.'

'We couldn't get along without you,' grunted Ilford sardonically. 'Let's have it.'

Laurence became businesslike. 'Positive identification on two sets of fingerprints from Herb Cullen's apartment. There's no way of dating them, but they belong to Sandy

Lang and this character Tank Lewis you asked Moss to check out.'

He paused, as if expecting applause. There was silence, and he shrugged.

'All right, the Freeman murder next. You know about the footprints at the car and among the trees. Freeman's prints are among the trees but not at the roadside. The woman and two men were at both places. We've clear prints – the woman is a size five, wide fitting – but until I get sample shoes for comparison, that's our lot there. The tyre marks are good. The tyres were near new, tread and track width are Continental. In other words, it has to be a foreign car – and I've got a list of possible models.' He anticipated Thane's question and grinned. 'Aye, one of them is an Alfa Romeo coupé.'

Ilford gave a nod of approval. 'Your turn, Doc. The autopsy reports?'

'Verbal, so far,' said the police surgeon apologetically. 'I only finished about an hour ago. Let's get the worst over first. Cullen's case is hopeless from a pathology viewpoint. All I can say is he died from multiple injuries, very multiple.'

'You warned us,' grunted llford. 'And Central Division made a muck of the thing when it came to getting witnesses – though I can't blame them completely. They saw it as an accident call at first, people do fall under trains now and again, and St. Enoch underground is a damned busy place. We could issue a newspaper appeal – but not yet, not when we're dealing with a man who almost certainly killed twice on one afternoon.' A fresh cloud of smoke billowed from his pipe. 'And Freeman?'

'Very different.' Doc Williams brightened. 'This heart man Milne came on the line about one a.m., and lectured me till I thought he'd never hang up. Then he kept calling back – it was like a return to dissection class at medical school.'

'I haven't had breakfast yet,' said Phil Moss uneasily. 'What about this "vagal inhibition" stuff?'

'Milne's right, and I might have missed it.' Doc Williams smiled in a way which made it clear he thought nothing of the kind. 'Milne suggested mechanical intervention at the main arteries of the neck – just here.' Finger and thumb went up to touch two spots at the front of his own throat. 'Get the exact pressure points, do it to a man with Freeman's cardiac background, and he'd be dead before you could say goodbye.' He looked down at his hand. 'Just a prod with finger and thumb, knowing what to do and where to do it – and no trace left unless you really know you're looking for it.'

'Finger and thumb.' Colin Thane repeated the words quietly. 'You're sure, Doc?'

Williams nodded. 'I found very slight bruising in the deep muscles of the neck, just where Milne suggested. We won't have final tissue samples till tomorrow – they need the wax-bath process and the rest. But I'm sure, Colin. If it's any consolation, Freeman wouldn't know it had happened.'

For a moment there was an awkward silence, then Moss spoke briskly.

'Millside contributions, sir. Tank Lewis and the woman Janey Milton that Hayes told us about. There's a link – they lived together for a spell and are still fairly friendly. You suggested Lewis for the Alhambra warehouse job, and it looks that way. He's suddenly spending money, a lot of it – and we've a lead through him to a couple of other neds with form.'

'Good,' growled Ilford. 'And the woman?'

'Records have her on file. Alias Elizabeth Vibor Quesson, age thirty-one. Originally Irish, drifted up from England about a year back, previous convictions for theft, embezzlement and assault.' Moss switched his gaze to the ceiling. 'She has a new transistor radio in her apartment and her shoes are size five, wide fitting – same as Super-intendent Laurence's footprint sample. I – well – per-suaded one of our tame neds to visit while she was out last night.'

'Breaking and entering.' Ilford spoke in a strangled voice. 'We didn't hear that, Moss. And if the Chief Con-stable did –' He swallowed and moved on quickly. 'Thane, I've had this mention of Barbar failing a police medical followed up. It's true. He failed on eyesight, like he said. But there's something else he didn't mention.' The next part obviously stuck in his throat. 'Not long after that, five years ago now, he won an official commendation for a citizen arrest. The man he brought in was a confidence trickster . . . Sandy Lang.'

'The start of a beautiful friendship!' Dan Laurence gave a chuckle one stage short of disbelief. 'That explains how he made his contacts – when he got round to this line of business, anyway.'

The telephone in the far corner of the room began ring-ing. Ilford waved the others to stay where they were, answered it, spoke briefly, then replaced the receiver.

'The other reason why we're here early,' he said cryp-tically, returning to his chair. 'I think this should help.'

In a moment there was a tap on the door. It opened and a burly, elderly man with a craggy face and a grey tweed suit came in.

'Ex-Sergeant Peters, Northern Division,' said Ilford crisply. 'Sergeant Peters retired two years back. He's now office supervisor with Barbar's agency.'

'And due at my desk at nine, sir,' reminded Peters wryly as the introductions were completed. 'It's bad enough asking me to work myself out of a reasonably good job, but worse if I'm going to be docked pay for being late!'

'This won't take long,' promised Ilford. He turned to the others. 'It riles me when an educated ned like Barbar uses ex-cops to set up his dirty little games. So why shouldn't we level the score a little – use the same men to help nail him? Sergeant Peters has been told a little of the situation. He's willing to help. Anyone object?'

Four heads shook as one, and Peters grinned.

'Tell me about the bank runs,' murmured Thane. 'Who's off sick just now?'

'Sick, sir?' Peters shrugged. 'Well, we do have a man off. But it's only a bit of a chill – he'd have come in except that Barbar told him to take a week off, full pay.'

'Is he usually so generous?'

'No – not with me, anyway.'

Moss gave a soft whistle which ended in a burp. Josh Barbar had made sure he'd a good reason for being involved in the bank van trips. A good reason, yet a simple one.

'And the night runs?' asked Ilford.

'Always casual, sir,' answered Peters. 'We might get one or two a week, but they rate as overtime.'

They talked to him for another couple of minutes, arranging details. When he left, it was after making a firm promise of regular reports.

As the door closed, Ilford knocked the ash from his pipe. 'Final details,' he announced briskly. 'We'll maintain shadowing routines all around. That includes a special watch on Barbar – we'll use a policewoman with a backup car in his case. Dan?'

'Tyres,' said Laurence lazily. 'The Alfa. I'll organize how it's done.'

'In my case, bed,' sighed Doc Williams. 'But if you need me, call.'

'Thane.'

'Among other things, the 3:40 bus to Fallside,' said Thane grimly. 'We'll try the crew first, then I'll put a team aboard this afternoon with photographs of the Milton woman and everyone else. I'm hoping for regular passengers who might remember faces. I've asked Records to run off copies of their C.R.O. file photographs. They'll distribute as fast as possible.'

'Then that's all for now,' declared Ilford. 'Except . . . well, just one thing, Colin.'

'Sir?'

'Make sure we run minimum risk as far as the bank is concerned.' Ilford sighed as he rose. 'I keep my account there. At the moment it's an overdraft.'

Chapter Seven

By eleven a.m. Colin Thane had tired of waiting. He left Headquarters with Moss in tow, found Erickson at the Millside duty car and travelled out to the Westpark district. They left the car three streets away from Jim Manneson's flat. Thane didn't expect The Tallyman bunch kept any real watch on the bank clerk's home, but there was no sense in a ceremonial arrival.

Splashing through the slush, they were snowballed by a tubby five-year-old at one corner and came near to colliding with a pram-pushing woman at the next. Moss trudged along, thin face pinched with cold, one shoe still leaking, stealing an occasional glance at the determined yet oddly relaxed figure by his side. Colin Thane seemed almost happy.

Perhaps because he was no longer grappling with shadows. Perhaps because Thane had begun the real gamble and knew the stakes.

It was up to them. Yet they weren't alone – no cop ever was when it reached this stage. Scattered around the city, few knowing more than their own immediate task, roughly twenty plain-clothes men and w.p.c.s were slogging through the same slush, ducking into doorways, occasionally retreating to the brief, welcome shelter of backup cars.

One team watched Sandy Lang from the moment he emerged, unshaven and dull-eyed, to eat breakfast at a truck-driver's cafe. A second watched Tank Lewis, who began his day by buying the racing papers. The third waited a long time before Janey Milton made her first appearance, on her way to have her hair set at a local beauty shop.

But the fourth team mattered most. Their target was Josh Barbar, their first terse report radioed back to Headquarters Control a little after nine a.m. when he left home driving the Alfa Romeo. Barbar motored quietly into the city, left the car in a parking lot a few hundred yards from his office, and walked the rest of the way. Dan Laurence noted that message, then drifted off to make his own arrangements.

The reports were still coming in, would keep on as long as contact was maintained. But so far the pattern gave no hint this Wednesday morning was anything more than the start to another cold, miserable January day.

At eleven-thirty, the latest report placed Josh Barbar as having joined the crew of his security truck on the start of its round. And the two Millside detectives toiled up the last few stairs to the apartment door which had 'J. Manneson' lettered in black on white plastic.

The girl who answered the doorbell's chime was pretty, slightly plump, and certainly not more than twenty. She wore a plain dress of grey wool, and for the rest Thane decided D. C. Beech's summing-up had been apt – 'the original dumb blonde except she's a redhead.' The red hair was cut short, framing an expression of childlike apprehension on a snub-nosed, wide-eyed face.

'Mrs Manneson?' asked Thane mildly.

'Yes.' Irene Manneson moistened her lips with a tiny red tip of tongue. 'If – if it's about the electricity –'

'Police.' He showed his warrant card. She scarcely glanced at it, fingertips rubbing together nervously, uncertain what to do.

138

Moss edged forward, clearing his throat. 'Mind if we come in?'

'Oh. No – I mean, yes.' The hands fluttered this time, then she gestured them in. 'It – it's a cold day. You must be nearly frozen.'

Once they'd entered she led the way through a tiny hallway into a room where the fitted carpet was near-new top-grade Wilton. But the chairs and a couch were old, faded, and obviously secondhand. A couple of bullfight posters from Spain, the type tourists and honeymooners bought as souvenirs, were framed on one wall. A tall standard lamp crowned by an elaborate, plum-coloured silk shade, had probably cost as much as the rest of the furniture put together.

The girl sensed their interest and flushed, the colour reaching up to the roots of her russet hair.

'We're waiting on a new suite arriving,' she said swiftly, defensively. 'What's here is – well, temporary. But sit down – most of it is comfortable.'

They did, and she perched herself on the edge of a leather-topped stool which had padding oozing out of one side.

'Mrs Manneson, my name is Thane. I'm a Chief Inspector with Millside Division C.I.D. This is Detective Inspector Moss.' He still wasn't quite sure how to tackle this one. 'You had a man at your door yesterday, asking questions about television programmes –'

'Him?' She relaxed a little and nodded, smiling. 'I gave him a cup of coffee. Though some of the things he said' – the smile switched to a giggle – 'well, I don't know how he gets away with it.' She stopped, suddenly alarmed. 'Is that why you're here? Has someone complained about him? I'm sure he didn't mean any harm.'

Moss fought down a twitch at the corner of his mouth, making a mental note that something would have to be done again about Beech before very much longer.

'Nobody has complained so far, Mrs Manneson. But he wasn't very interested in TV. He was a police officer.'

'He *was?*' She blinked, puzzled, then the worry broke through again. 'Then why did he come here? If it's something we haven't paid –' Her voice died away.

'And that could be quite a few things, couldn't it, Mrs Manneson?' Try as he might, Thane couldn't shut all of the pity from his voice. 'Furniture, food, and now I'd guess it is the electricity bill. How far has it gone? Expecting the power to be cut off any moment?'

The girl gnawed her lip and nodded, frightened now. 'But we've – well, we haven't done anything to involve the police, Chief Inspector. And Jim says everything will be all right soon, as long as we don't get into more trouble.' She rocked back and forward a little, tears not far from her eyes. 'I haven't bought anything, I haven't signed anything for ages now.'

'You're sure?' Thane glanced significantly towards the standard lamp.

'That was a wedding present.' Irene Manneson's chin came up a little. 'We got it from the bank.'

'Bank clerks aren't particularly well paid,' mused Moss, taking his turn. 'It's a steady job, of course. Good prospects – and they seem to think a lot of your husband. But banks don't like their staff getting into debt.'

'I know.' It came like a whisper.

Thane leaned forward, the old wood of the chair creaking beneath his weight. 'Mrs Manneson, did Jim say why everything would soon be all right?'

'He's doing some extra work, helping with a firm's books or something. They're going to pay him when the job's done. I – I've taken a part-time job too.'

Thane sighed a little to himself. 'Does The Tallyman mean anything to you, Mrs Manneson?'

She frowned, then shook her head.

140

'But you've had the Barbar debt-collection people round?'

'Yes.' Her voice still trembled. 'They worked out how much we could pay a week, and the man comes on Fridays.' The doorbell chimed and she jerked upright from the stool. 'If that's the electricity people –'

'Then we'll chase them,' Thane told her firmly. 'Answer it. But if it is anyone else, don't tell them we're here and don't let them in – whatever the reason.'

The doorbell chimed again, more insistently. Irene Manneson sighed and left the room. They heard the main door open, followed by the brief murmur of voices. Then the door closed again and she returned.

'He' – she glanced over her shoulder – 'he said it would be all right, Chief Inspector.'

'Hello, sir!' D.C. Beech came in, grinning cheerfully. 'Headquarters sent me over with a progress report. We tried the house phone number but couldn't get through.'

Irene Manneson moved her feet uncomfortably. 'It was cut off last month.'

'Who needs a telephone anyway?' Beech shrugged his unconcern. 'Anyway, old Buddha – I mean the Chief Superintendent thought I was the best candidate for the job. People know my face around here.'

'From what I've heard, they're likely to remember it,' said Thane with a dry, partly wasted sarcasm. He switched his attention back to the girl. 'Mrs Manneson, we're going to be here for a while. Why not make yourself a cup of coffee? Phil, you'll give her a hand, won't you?'

Moss smothered a mumble of protest, hauled himself out of his chair, and guided her off towards the kitchen.

'Well?' Thane glanced at Beech. 'What have you got?'

'This, sir.' Beech reached into an inside pocket and produced an envelope. 'Oh, and photographs. The set Records have turned out.' They were in another, bulkier envelope.

141

Thane took them and glanced briefly at the photographs. They were the usual C.R.O. full-face and side-on views, one each for Sandy Lang, Tank Lewis and the Milton woman. Lewis was a square-faced thug with a scar above one eye. Janey Milton had too small a mouth and too big a nose to be called good-looking. He laid them aside, lit a cigarette, and opened the other envelope.

The report had been prepared in a hurry, badly typed and with the last few paragraphs added in a hasty ink scrawl. As Thane read it through, a thin smile began gathering at the corners of his mouth.

It was firming now, firming in all directions.

Barbar was still out with the security van, and the watch on the others had produced no surprises.

But the rest began with Dan Laurence's team. The Scientific Bureau squad had checked the Alfa Romeo, still lying in the car park. The tyre treads matched up with the impressions found at Fallside – not in terms strong enough to satisfy a court of law, but sufficient to load the odds against them being wrong.

Inside Barbar's office, ex-Sergeant Peters was making good his promises. He'd telephoned that Josh Barbar had announced he was taking the next few days off. And the moment Barbar had left with the security truck Peters had raided his way through the agency files – which showed Jim Manneson making a five-pound-a-week repayment on credit-store debts totalling close on four hundred pounds.

Equally important – maybe more so because it firmly tied her in – photographs of Janey Milton had been identified by the Fallside bus conductor. The little Pakistani was positive the blonde had been a passenger.

The last was small, inconclusive, yet with its own satisfaction for Central Division, still smarting under their slow start on Herb Cullen's death.

They had a new witness, the first worth any real attention. Most of the credit belonged to a St. Enoch ticket collector. When a woman passenger had talked to him that morning he'd telephoned Central C.I.D. straight away. The woman had been behind Cullen in the queue to purchase tickets. He'd been talking to a man whom she vaguely remembered as having long hair and glasses – and it was Cullen's companion who bought the tickets before they headed down towards the trains.

Carefully, Thane folded the sheet and put it away.

'Will I head back now?' asked Beech.

'Not for a spell.' Thane glanced round as Irene Manneson returned with coffee on a tray, Moss at her heels. He beckoned her over and fanned out the photographs.

'Ever seen any of them, Mrs Manneson?'

She peered at them, and he realized she was probably shortsighted. But she nodded a moment later.

'The woman – that's Miss Milton. She – she loans money.'

'She loaned some to you?'

'Yes. She came to the door one day and I – well, I arranged it with her.' Her face twisted unhappily. 'Jim didn't like it.'

'How much of a loan?' He saw a start of stubborn reluctance and his voice hardened. 'Mrs Manneson, how much?'

'I don't have to tell you,' she protested, small fists clenching. 'You – I don't even know why you're here!'

'Among other things we're here to keep your husband out of the biggest trouble he's ever likely to land in,' snapped Thane. Unless, he added mentally, Manneson one day reached the stage of trying to wring his wife's neck. 'How much, Mrs Manneson?'

'A hundred pounds.' Something much more urgent at last came to her mind. 'I want to know. Has something happened to Jim?'

'Not yet – and the rest depends on him.' Abruptly, Thane

brought her back to what mattered. 'Who's repaying the loan – your husband?'

'Yes. Miss Milton wanted it that way.'

Time passed. Irene Manneson began to prepare lunch, resolutely setting the table for two. Leaning near the doorway, watching her, Moss winced as his ulcer stabbed with its usual punctuality. He belched, drew himself in a little, and quickly lit one of the herbal mixtures. In a matter of moments he felt even worse and stubbed it out.

The girl glanced at him, then went back to the kitchen. When she reappeared she handed him a glass of milk. She'd gone again before he could thank her. Moss began sipping, deciding the worst part was when people tried hard to be kind.

The room clock ticked past noon. Then, stationed at the window, Beech murmured a warning.

'Manneson, sir.'

'Alone?' asked Thane, straightening up.

'Looks like it.' Beech stayed where he was.

Jim Manneson let himself in with his key. They didn't stop the red-haired girl as she rushed to meet him but waited, hearing the couple talking quickly and urgently.

At last Manneson came through, stopping just inside the room, his wife at his side. His face was pale, making the purple weal around the right side of his mouth stand out clearer than ever. He looked at them one by one and gave a twitch of recognition as he reached Thane.

'You want to see me?' The words came with a forced attempt at confidence.

'That's right.' Thane got to his feet and beckoned Beech over from the window. 'Take Mrs Manneson through to the kitchen – she'll want to keep that meal heated for a spell. Phil, keep an eye on the street.'

Without protest the girl let herself be led out. As the

144

door closed, Thane nodded to the fair-haired bank clerk. 'Sit down.'

'I would anyway. It's my house,' reminded Manneson defiantly. He took a chair, carefully watching his trouser creases. 'Another thing, I don't like coming home and finding Irene half-scared out of her wits. What's it all about?'

'I'll show you,' said Thane grimly, standing over him. He tossed the photographs into Manneson's lap. 'Take a look at these.'

One glance was enough. He froze.

'It really comes down to a single question,' murmured Thane, gathering the photographs and returning them to his pocket. 'When do they raid the bank?'

Manneson jerked as if stung. 'I don't know what you mean!'

'Don't be too hasty, laddie,' cautioned Moss from the window, his voice quiet in its warning. 'Colin, we've company out there.'

Thane gripped Manneson's arm, pulled him to his feet, and nodded towards the window. 'Let's take a look. But don't try anything – you'd regret it.'

They joined Moss in the shelter of the curtains and glanced down. A thin, bearded figure, hands deep in the pockets of a heavy overcoat, stood in a doorway a few yards down on the other side of the street.

'Sandy Lang – and he looks damned cold.' Moss chuckled. 'Now look further down. See a woman with a shopping bag?'

Manneson nodded silently. The woman was about a hundred yards along the street, gazing into a shop window.

'If you're interested, her name is Abigail MacDonald,' murmured Thane. 'She's a policewoman, despite the shopping bag. Lang's watching you, she's watching Lang – like we're watching them all.' He paused, then added deliberately. 'Including Josh Barbar.'

The reaction, when it came, wasn't what he'd expected.

'Who – who's Barbar?'

Thane shrugged, brought Manneson back from the window, and pushed him back into the same chair.

'You admit you know the others?'

'Yes.' It came like a sigh.

'But not Barbar? Slim build, long, reddish hair, wears glasses?'

'There's a man who comes to the bank,' began Manneson uncertainly. 'I've seen him, but that's all. He's with a security firm.'

'Forget it.' Thane kept the disappointment from his voice. 'Let's save some time, Manneson. We know The Tallyman has his hooks in you. And that was a pretty good story you told your boss about your face. But he wasn't the one who saw you in that alley after Herb Cullen roughed you up.'

'You mean it was – it was you who came along?' Manneson swallowed a groan.

'I didn't get much chance to go into introductions,' said Thane, grinning a little. 'Back to the question. We saw Lang trying that key in the main door last night. So when does it happen?'

'You know just about everything else, don't you?' Manneson ran a trembling, apprehensive hand across his face. Then, suddenly, he looked up. 'Or *do* you, do you really?'

'I think so.' Thane switched to a more sympathetic key. 'Most of it, anyway, Jim. Enough to know how The Tallyman puts on pressure.' He took out his cigarettes, gave Manneson one, and noted the slight shake in the bank clerk's hand as he accepted a light.

'Do they know at the bank?' asked Manneson, his voice little more than a whisper. 'Was that why you were there yesterday?'

'No.' Thane sat down opposite him. 'Not yet, though it'll

146

have to happen. But there are other jobs – once you get The Tallyman off your back. How long has it been?'

'Five months.' The bank clerk stared bleakly at the carpet for a second. 'It shouldn't have happened – and it wasn't just Irene's fault. I work with money. I should have kept us on a budget.'

'Too much week at the end of the money,' mused Thane. 'It happens to plenty of people. How tough did The Tallyman's neds shape?'

Manneson bit his lip. 'Tough enough to say Irene wouldn't look so good if she got acid on her face. I – I decided they meant it.'

Thane said nothing, knowing it was best. But a swift catalogue flickered through his mind, the kind of violence the city had tasted when thugs put on pressures. A gelignite bomb in a windowsill at one of the new housing blocks in the Gorbals. When it exploded, two children were blown across a room. The man stabbed to death in an armchair while his wife watched. The other bomb wired to a car's turn indicator. The razor-slashed. The maimed. All the others. Violence came cheaply for even the lowest stakes.

Sometimes for no stake at all.

'Chief Inspector, it's tonight.' The words came quietly. 'They've got keys to the main door and the basement area. I've to knock out the alarm system before I leave this evening.'

'How?'

'It's easy enough – the system's so old it was probably wired by Noah. And they gave me a little thing like a clock. Clip it on, and it kills the system between eleven and one a.m., but leaves things working normally the rest of the time.'

'And they're going to try for that strong-room?' Thane frowned dubiously.

Manneson laughed, a chilling, tired laugh which seemed

147

to echo in the room. 'That means you don't know quite as much as I thought, Mr Thane.'

'We're always willing to listen,' said Moss, easing back from his post at the window. 'Lang's moved – he's heading up the street. We can forget him for a spell.'

Thane nodded absently, his attention fixed on the young, bitterly confident figure in front of him. 'Tell me about tonight,' he invited.

'It has to be tonight,' declared Manneson. Ash dropped from his cigarette and quickly, almost guiltily, he rubbed it underfoot until it vanished into the carpet. 'Every Scottish bank issues its own bank notes, correct?'

Thane nodded again, with a trace of impatience. There were five Scottish bank groups, each issuing their own notes, each issue accepted national currency. Visitors found it confusing, but the practice came down to jealously guarded historical accident.

'Bank notes wear out – they get torn, dirty, damaged,' explained Manneson, the words coming hesitantly at first, then swiftly. 'At all our branches the counter staff keep withdrawing old Central Scotland notes from circulation – other banks do the same for their issues. The old notes come to head office in bundles, and whatever is collected is destroyed once every three months.'

'How?' demanded Moss.

'They're fed through a machine like a mincer, then the scraps are burned on the spot.'

Thane frowned. 'I saw something like a stove in the basement – a big, ugly-looking thing.'

'That's the one.' Manneson drew a deep breath. 'The job's always done by four people, all top management – Mr Daill's one of them. As far as they're concerned, it's a quarterly fun night. The rest of the staff are gone, they start off with a full-scale dinner in the boardroom about eight – drinks, the lot – then get down to burning the money about eleven.'

148

'Sounds like an orgy,' grinned Moss, scratching his chin and envy in his voice. 'I'll bet they use ten-pound notes to light the cigars.'

'Or dud cheques,' grimaced Thane. 'All right, Jim, how much old money will they get rid of tonight?'

'Last time it was about a hundred and sixty – thousand, that is. This time it'll be more. There's always extra money in circulation over Christmas and New Year, and it gets a lot of handling.' Manneson drew hard on the cigarette. 'It's a guess, Mr Thane. But I'd say over two hundred thousand.'

'Two hundred thousand . . .' Colin Thane stopped, then cursed in a slow, deliberate fashion which raised Moss's eyebrows in frank admiration. Then he leaned forward, frowning. 'How does The Tallyman reckon on getting to it? What about those cage doors – how can he get past that second one, the remote-control job?'

'They've already done it twice,' countered Manneson dully. 'They took me along the first time, about a month ago – just to make sure. From the front door into the vault took two minutes and twenty-eight seconds. Lang says they did better the second time.'

'Rehearsals –' Moss almost choked on the word. 'You mean it?'

'Uh-huh.' Manneson licked his lips. 'I got impressions of the keys for them first – that was easy enough. I'm early staff, which means helping to open up. And if you know where to look there's an outside control which overrides the remote switch on the lower door. It's a safety measure.'

For Colin Thane, the world seemed to be going mad. A haul of used notes, impossible to trace. A raid with keys, with the alarm system knocked out – a raid already rehearsed right down into the bank vault.

'Isn't there a ruddy night watchman?'

'Old Charlie,' nodded Manneson. 'He always has his tea break just after eleven. He uses a room up on the top floor.

149

You could haul the whole bank from under him and he wouldn't know.'

Thane swallowed hard, trying to hold on to reality. 'Mind telling me where *you* fit in tonight – apart from fixing the alarm system?'

'I – I don't.' Manneson sounded almost apologetic for the fact. 'I've to stay home. And – well, I just won't hear from them again.' He drew a deep, unhappy breath. 'At least, that's how it was going to be, Mr Thane. I suppose – I suppose you'll want to charge me now.'

Colin Thane exchanged a long glance with Moss. The latter's face remained expressionless, but he already knew the decision was made.

'Go and get fed,' said Thane wearily. 'Then get back to your damned bank on time.'

'But' – Manneson's mouth fell open.

'Do what you're told. Say nothing to anyone, and fix that alarm exactly as you were going to – that's an order.' Thane got to his feet, knowing this might mean burning the last of several boats. 'As of this moment you're under police protection as a Crown witness. But play it straight, I'm warning you.'

A sudden hope had flared in the fair-haired youngster's eyes. Then it wavered a little.

'What – what about Irene?'

'I'll leave a man here – from now till it's over.'

'And – and the bank?'

Moss gave a grunt of irritation. 'Hell, laddie, you can't have it all ways. Yes or no?'

Manneson gave a slow, resolute nod.

'Tell me one thing,' said Thane suddenly. 'That night at the Lombok Club – what was the idea?'

'I thought I'd worked out a system,' said Manneson glumly. 'If it had paid off, Irene and I would have been on the next plane to anywhere. I'd even got the passports.'

'There's only one foolproof system for roulette,' said

Thane, his voice sinking to a low, musing reminiscence. 'And I only know one man who used it.'

'Did – did he win a lot?' queried Manneson hopefully.

'Not a penny, son. But he didn't lose.' Thane pursed his lips for a moment, then thumbed towards the door. 'Now, get moving.'

Leaving the apartment at his usual time, still slightly pale of face but otherwise his apparent normal self, Jim Manneson caught a bus at the corner of the street and arrived back at the bank exactly at the end of his lunch break.

Sandy Lang followed him, using a cream-coloured Ford Cortina as transport. And following Lang in turn came the other watchers, radioing at intervals to Headquarters Control.

Before Manneson reached the bank Colin Thane was already on his way again. Leaving Beech on guard at the apartment, he walked back to the duty car with Moss. They made a fast trip to Headquarters, then, while Moss went to check the latest reports at Control, Thane plunged into a long session with Buddha Ilford.

This time their conference was in a corner of the Head-quarters canteen, where Ilford had been finishing lunch. Thane ordered stew, talked as he ate, and had the mild satisfaction of seeing the C.I.D. chief lose all interest in the rest of his meal.

'Two hundred thousand –' Ilford turned a pastel shade of purple, and gave a rumbling growl which made two visiting detective inspectors leave quicker than they'd intended. 'You know what's going to happen if anything goes wrong?'

'I've an idea, sir.' Thane mopped up the last of the stew and flourished his fork for emphasis. 'But we need it this way. Otherwise, how much real evidence have we got against any of them?'

'Enough for some charges.' Ilford scowled and dragged

151

out his pipe. He sucked hard on the stem, ignoring the empty bowl. 'I know, not the kind of charges that matter. And you've no guarantee that Josh Barbar will be in on the raid. Damn it, how can he be there and up at Glen Craig at the same time?'

'That's the one problem left,' admitted Thane. 'Still, I might go round to his office and – well, more or less ask him. He might be surprised to see me.'

For a moment Ilford stared at him as if he'd gone mad. Then he nodded. 'Why not? It makes about as much sense as anything else. You think Manneson will do what you've told him?'

'That's my gamble, sir.' And with a lot more than even Ilford realized at stake, Thane told himself wryly. 'He knows it amounts to his one chance.'

'Just *his?*' Ilford's lower lip quivered a little. 'I'd be a lot happier if the bank bosses knew what was going on. Even now we're leaving it late.'

'I'd like to leave it until the place has closed, sir,' mused Thane. 'Try to time it for just about when they're sitting down to that meal.'

Ilford sighed. 'I always knew there was a nice, peasant-style sadistic streak hidden inside you, Colin.'

Thane grinned, knowing he'd won.

'You'll be around, sir?'

'I wouldn't miss it for anything,' said Ilford with a wasted sarcasm. 'Remember, it could be my funeral as well as yours. Where's Moss?'

'Catching up on things.' Thane pushed back his chair. 'He'll be looking in for something to eat.'

He was outside the building, looking for the duty car, before he realized he left Ilford to pay for both meals. It was the kind of little touch which would reduce the C.I.D. chief to a final frenzy.

The Barbar Agency office was located in a quiet street

down near the river. What had once been a shop front had been painted over with a king-sized variation of the agency's lion crest, but an old shop-style bell still clanged as Thane pushed his way through the glass door.

Inside, he found a long counter, a few chairs and a couple of shabbily dressed women paying money to a teen-age clerkess, who had a strawberry-pink lipstick and a spotty complexion. She took the cash, entered the payments in record cards, then smiled at him as the women went out.

He asked for Barbar, waited while she rang through on a house phone to one of the office rooms, at the rear, and grinned a little as he heard his name being repeated to the voice at the other end of the wire.

The girl put the telephone down. 'He's just coming, Chief Inspector.'

Thane thanked her. The shop bell clanged again and another woman came in, money and payment card ready. He wondered to himself how much she owed, how it had happened, then shrugged. It always happened to someone. Probably it always would.

'Hello, Thane!' Barbar's voice brought him round. The man was standing at a doorway wearing country tweeds and heavy brogue shoes in place of his usual city-style clothes. The smile on his face was slightly forced, his manner wary. 'What brings you round?'

'Curiosity – and that invitation you gave me,' said Thane smoothly.

'Good. Come on through.' Barbar showed quick resilience. The smile broadened as he lifted a wooden counterflap and Thane squeezed through. 'Smooth journey back last night?'

'No.' Thane grimaced, following him beyond the partition into a general office. 'Some idiot blinded me off the road on a bend, then kept on going.'

'Bad luck.' Barbar gave an appropriate murmur of sympathy. 'How's the car?'

'Being hauled back on the road about now, I think.' There were two people at desks in the room. One was a typist, frowning over her machine, the other was ex-Sergeant Peters. The retired cop gave no sign of recognition.

'Not a lot to see, I'm afraid,' said Barbar almost apologetically. 'Most of my boys are out most of the day, on house-to-house stuff. Still, here's someone you may know, the staff supervisor.'

He introduced Peters. Thane frowned and shook his head. 'We've met somewhere, Sergeant. But I can't place it.'

'I did some plain-clothes work a few years back,' said Peters, equally polite. 'Maybe it was then.' He turned to Barbar. 'Anything for the security van tonight, sir?'

'No, we won't need it. I'll see you soon about coping with the next few days.' Barbar nodded to the man and led Thane through to his private office, a cubbyhole of a room.

'Like a drink while you're here?' he asked.

'Haven't time, I'm afraid,' said Thane. The room boasted a small TV set and cocktail cabinet, but there was no shade on the light bulb. 'I really looked in to see if you'd take a message for me to Doctor Milne. You're still going up there today?'

'Uh-huh. Leaving about five, if I'm lucky.' Barbar removed his spectacles and began cleaning them with one corner of a handkerchief. 'What's the message?'

'Just that I've managed to smooth the formalities about Harry Freeman's death and that he's got my thanks for his help.'

Barbar's eyes, watery without the lenses, flickered. Then he nodded. 'I'll tell him. That's all?'

'Yes.' Thane glanced at his watch. 'Well, I'd better move. But have a good time up there.'

'I usually do.' Barbar piloted him back through the office area to the main counter. 'And I hope the car isn't too badly bent.'

'That makes two of us,' said Thane wryly.

Outside, as the shop door clanged shut behind him, he glanced around before climbing back into the duty car. A small red Mini was parked about a hundred yards along the road. The windows were steamed up.

Thane grinned. Josh Barbar was being watched more closely than any goldfish in a bowl.

Millside Division took on a particular atmosphere when the waiting time came round. A stranger wouldn't notice much. The front office performed the usual tasks, booked its drunks, dealt with old ladies and lost dogs, kept its usual chatter of teleprinter links and buzz of radio traffic.

But upstairs, in the C.I.D. room, there were more than the usual number of men around – day shift staying late, night shift pulled in early. The unlucky ones were dispatched on routine jobs, the others waited, smoked, drank tea, argued half-heartedly about football, and watched the door of Colin Thane's room.

By four-thirty when Chief Superintendent Ilford arrived from Headquarters, the tension was mounting. Moments later, Phil Moss came out. He looked around, gave a gargantuan belch, and returned to the room again.

The d.c.s grinned. What they'd do with Moss and his ulcer was a topic which lasted another half hour.

Inside the room, things were different. Buddha Ilford had contented himself with a seat by the window. Relaxed behind his desk, Colin Thane looked as though he hadn't a worry in the world – except that he was smoking twice his usual amount and jerked upright each time the telephone rang.

'I wonder,' said Ilford suddenly, half to himself.

'Sir?' Moss turned from the crime map. He'd been quietly moving a few pins around, hoping Ilford hadn't spotted they were still behind on occurrence plotting.

'I wonder about Barbar.' Ilford gave a pensive frown. 'If he'd passed that police medical – and he entered, I checked – if he'd made the force, how would he have shaped?'

'I can guess,' said Thane cynically. 'We'd have a bent cop on our hands, sir. As bent as a corkscrew at a convention.'

'Maybe.' The C.I.D. chief pondered the point. They left him to it. Ever since the Chief Constable had packed Buddha off to a series of lectures on criminal psychology, he was liable to launch into a theory about cause and effect. Usually he ended up in a foul temper.

Thane exchanged a faint wink with Phil Moss and turned again to the last batch of reports teleprinted in from Control.

They were still unexciting. Barbar was at his office, Tank Lewis had gone home, Janey Milton had met up with Sandy Lang in the centre of town and both had disappeared into the nearest bar.

But he wondered how the quartet would have reacted to the separate, typewritten sheet on his desk, the report by the C.I.D. team who'd invaded the 3:40 p.m. Fallside bus. Three regular passengers had identified Janey Milton's photograph and remembered Harry Freeman. One, a mechanic who'd been interested in Janey Milton's legs, had seen her heading towards a parked car at the terminus. And his interest had switched sufficiently from woman to car to confirm it had been an Alfa.

The other photographs had met with no response. If Janey Milton had been escorted by a 'minder,' then he was someone still not on the list.

And that wasn't quite all. Detective Sergeant MacLeod was plodding around dockland, following up a tip that the crew of a Danish freighter had been offered a bargain line in transistor radios – provided they bought in bulk.

The phone rang again. He lifted it, answered shortly, then replaced the receiver.

'Well?' Ilford raised an eyebrow.

'Check call, sir,' he explained briefly. 'I had the phone people reopen the line to Manneson's apartment – just in case.'

'Good.' Ilford looked at his watch. 'I suggest we get down to the radio room. If anything's going to happen it should be soon.'

They moved. Down on the ground floor, the uniformed communications sergeant faced the invasion with a wary good humour and placed them well away from his precious equipment.

For long, crawling minutes there was nothing but a hiss of static from the radio tuned to the shadow cars' frequency. Then, suddenly, it burst into life.

At 4:55 Car Fox-Able reported Sandy Lang had moved and now had his car parked outside the Bank of Central Scotland.

At 5:01 the bank staff began to leave.

At 5:04 Car Dog-Victor reported Josh Barbar walking from his office towards the parking lot.

At 5:06 Jim Manneson left the bank. He nodded to Lang, then headed for his bus. Fox-Able passed another message moments later. Lang was back in his Ford and was driving towards the riverside.

Dog-Victor came to life again at 5:11. Barbar was in his car, but hadn't moved from the parking lot.

Another two minutes, then both call signs reported. Sandy Lang's Ford had arrived at the parking lot. He climbed out, crossed over to Barbar's car, spoke to him at the window, then went back to the Ford.

At 5:14 Fox-Able reported Lang heading for home.

At 5:16 Dog-Victor was trailing behind Barbar's Alfa Romeo as it began travelling north out of town.

'And that's that.' Buddha Ilford gave a long sigh. 'Well, still think Barbar's going to be in on the job?'

'I'll stick at "no comment",' said Thane stubbornly. He confirmed that communications would feed them any further signals, then led the way back to his room.

The telephone was ringing as they entered. Moss scooped up the receiver, answered, then turned to Ilford.

'For you, sir – Peters, from the Barbar office.'

Ilford took the phone. For the next few minutes the C.I.D. chief's end of the conversation came down to a series of grunts and an occasional, sharp 'You're sure?'

At last, he hung up.

'Peters, like you said.' He smacked his lips with satisfaction. 'A thorough man. He's just leaving for the night, but he went through Barbar's office first, including the desk. He's – ah – rather apologetic about forcing the lock, particularly as he found damn all of any worth inside. On the other hand, the wastepaper basket was interesting. He found a receipt there, date-stamped today, for six gallons of diesel fuel.'

If he expected a reaction, he was disappointed.

'Diesel fuel,' repeated Ilford, sighing his impatience. 'Barbar's security truck has a diesel engine. The usual routine is for the fuel tank to be topped up in the morning, by Peters. The truck's kept in a shed behind their office and he checked – the tank's already filled. Ask yourself why.'

It got home. Thane whistled softly. 'If you're going to raid a bank, you need transport. And who'd think there was anything strange in a security truck stopped outside a bank, even at night?'

'But it doesn't fit,' frowned Moss. 'It would mean Barbar

sticking his neck right out, and he hasn't done that before.'

'He'd still be in the clear if somebody stole the truck from that shed.' Thane felt a touch of admiration for the coolness involved. 'Barbar's far away, someone pinches his vehicle – give him full marks. It's smooth.'

Odd puffing noises came from Buddha Ilford's lips. He got to his feet, padded over to the window, and looked out into the night and the scattered lights of the surrounding tenements. The white mantle of snow on their roofs gave a pale unreality to the scene, hid the dirt and poverty they represented.

'That's it, then,' he growled at last. 'I'm not waiting any longer. We contact the bank. Thane –'

'Sir?' Thane guessed what was coming and knew he'd only himself to blame.

'You shaped it – so you explain it. The man to contact will be Patterson Daill, their general manager. I've got his direct-line phone number.' Ilford reached towards an inside pocket.

'We know him, sir. And the number,' said Moss confidently. 'At least – that's right, isn't it, Colin?'

'Yes.' Thane said it flatly.

'Oh.' Ilford blinked a little.

'We're that kind of a division, sir,' said Moss with a righteous humility.

Thane made a last try. 'It still might come better from you, sir.'

Ilford shook his head and turned his attention to filling his pipe.

Slowly, Thane lifted the telephone, gave the station switchboard the number, and waited. The phone at the other end rang for a full half-minute before it was answered.

'Yes?' Crisply cheerful, Patterson Daill's voice echoed over the wire.

159

'Thane, Millside C.I.D. –'

'Ah!' Daill didn't let him go on. 'I was just talking about you to some colleagues, Thane. Something I can help you with? Little problems can crop up when decisions have to be made.'

'It's an official call,' said Thane, feeling suddenly hoarse. 'I have Chief Superintendent Ilford with me at the moment.'

'I see.' Daill's manner made it very plain he didn't. In the background, Thane could hear other voices and laughter.

'We have information an attempt will be made to raid the bank tonight. It will be sometime between eleven and one, while you're destroying the old bank notes.'

'While we're . . .' Daill's voice rose to a strangled squeak. He said something quickly and sharply to the other people at his end of the line and the background noises suddenly ended. 'Thane, if this is some kind of a joke I'm not particularly amused!'

'I'm not in a comedy mood, Mr Daill,' said Thane bitterly. He saw Ilford strike a match, then watched him as the first blue smoke began to rise from the pipebowl. 'You're going to have visitors. They've had inside help, they've got keys, your alarm system will be out of action, they know exactly where to go and what to do.'

The silence on the line was more eloquent than any words. Then the bank executive spoke again with a new geniality.

'Excellent! You've proved what we believed, Thane! So now you'll arrest these villains, nip the whole thing in the bud, eh?'

'No, sir.' Thane drew a deep breath. 'That's exactly what we're not going to do.'

'What?' The exclamation beat against his ear like a minor explosion.

'We intend to nail them in the act, inside the bank.' He

saw Ilford give a happy nod. 'It needs a little cooperation on your part, Mr Daill.'

'Cooperation? Thane, this bank is a major institution. You – you're on the brink of becoming an officer of the company. I forbid any action which could bring adverse publicity in our direction. Think of the effect on public confidence, man!'

Thane sighed. 'Mr Daill, what if I told you they've already rehearsed this – that they've already been inside the bank at least once during the night?' He didn't wait for an answer. 'Unless we do it this way we can't be certain of catching them all. We can't be certain of having enough evidence.'

'No?' It came like a groan. Then, after a pause, Daill asked sharply, 'Thane, how long have you known about this? It – a situation of this type doesn't shape in five minutes.'

'We've been working on it,' he admitted cautiously. Ilford had a grin behind the pipesmoke. Moss's face was tightly expressionless. 'We had to be sure first, and we had to make certain we didn't scare them off.'

'So you leave it till now.' It crackled over the line like a condemnation. 'You've deliberately avoided warning us, exposed the bank to – to this danger. Well, it's going to require considerable explanation. Not just to me. To my board, Thane.'

The threat in the words couldn't have been spelled out clearer, but Thane brushed it aside. 'That can wait, the rest can't. Are you going to help?'

'We don't appear to have any option.' Daill's voice was cold but resigned.

They got down to details. The smoothest way to get a squad into the bank building unseen was via a top-floor fire-escape bridge which led from the next building. Reluctantly, Daill accepted that and the rest.

At last, Thane put down the receiver.

'It's fixed,' he said wryly.

'Good.' Ilford regarded him with a touch of curiosity. 'You seem to know Daill fairly well. At least –' He stopped as there was a knock on the door. The duty orderly came in, laid down a message form, and waited.

Ilford glanced at it, shrugged, and shoved it across the desk. Car Dog-Victor had lost touch with Barbar's car. The Alfa Romeo had vanished from the main north road while the police unit was delayed in traffic.

'I want county forces between here and Glen Craig alerted,' said Ilford heavily. 'No contact requested. Just sighting reports.'

The orderly nodded and went out.

'What was I saying?' Ilford pursed his lips, then shrugged. 'It doesn't matter. I'll get back to Headquarters and talk to a few people. I want to make sure nothing goes wrong. It – ah – might be unfortunate if it did.'

'And Barbar, sir?' queried Moss.

'He'll turn up – one place or the other.' Ilford headed for the door, then stopped. 'Any problems, Thane?'

'No, sir,' said Colin Thane.

And hoped it sounded as if he meant it.

Chapter Eight

'My God,' said Patterson Daill, making the words a prayer. 'If anything goes wrong . . .'

He was in his shirt-sleeves, half-naked by Bank of Central Scotland standards. He had liquor on his breath and despair written across his plump red face.

'Everything's ready,' soothed Colin Thane. 'And when it's over you'll be a hero. Think what it'll do for customer relations.'

'The Board doesn't approve of heroes,' said Daill almost petulantly. He turned on his heel and went sadly across the basement to rejoin the three other bank executives who formed the official money-burning party.

Colin Thane grinned and lit a cigarette. A few feet away the oil-fired incinerator furnace purred softly. Beside it, the milling machine had the covers removed to show its glinting, hungry steel jaws. The main-vault door was closed, guarded by its complex of locks. But a smaller safe, man-high, lay open. The bank quartet had already dragged its contents into the cold glare of the basement's tube lights. Neatly packaged in lots of five thousand, not far short of a quarter-million pounds in used notes lay waiting destruction.

The guard grille at the foot of the stairway creaked open. Phil Moss came in, nodded to the detective controlling the remote switch, and walked over rubbing his hands.

'Everybody in position,' he said cheerfully.

'Good,' nodded Thane. He knew the details by heart but went over them again, probably for the twentieth time. They had twelve plain-clothes men in the bank, an observation post high in an office block on the other side of the street, six cars carefully hidden around the immediate area.

The bank's usual night guard, an ex-army corporal whose medals stopped a couple of wars back, had been left to watch the top-floor fire-escape bridge. That had been Moss's idea. It gave the old soldier something to do and kept him well out of harm's way.

Most of the police squad were now concealed around the ground floor. The others – Thane looked around. He had one d.c. operating a radio link with a handset, the man by the grille switch and two others.

'Who's running our lookout?' queried Moss.

'Dan Laurence. He's trying out some new toy, an infrared camera or something.'

The grille squeaked open again. Chief Superintendent Ilford had arrived. He stopped inside the basement, inspected the scene for a moment, then beckoned the two Millside men over.

As they joined him, he dragged a pair of Service-pattern Webley .38s from his overcoat pockets and handed them over. 'I signed for these myself – so don't lose the damned things.'

'Aye.' Moss frowned at the gun in his hand, then tucked it into his trouser waistband. 'Your idea, sir?'

'In part,' qualified Ilford.

Guns were rarely issued in any Scottish force. When they were, it needed high-up approval and the issue was limited.

'How many, sir?' asked Thane quietly.

'Another here,' said Ilford, patting his pocket. 'I left two upstairs, with a couple of the Central men. Usual instruction – limited to emergency use.' He glanced around again,

164

curious. 'Which of them is Daill? I don't know him by sight.'

'The one in shirt-sleeves,' Thane told him. 'He's – well, still a little bit upset.'

'You surprise me,' grunted Ilford, then chuckled. 'I've just come from Dan Laurence. Now there's someone who seems really happy. He's sitting three floors up with enough junk to stock a warehouse. Long-focus camera, coupled infrared searchlight, batteries, viewers –' He shook his head. 'His bunch claim they can get portrait-style enlargements up to a hundred-yards range in pitch darkness.'

'I'll order half a dozen,' said Thane dryly. 'We've a little present for him here when it's over.'

'This alarm-system interrupter?' Ilford raised a quizzical eyebrow. 'What's it like?'

'A clockwork mechanism triggering a bypass switch of some kind.' Thane rubbed a hand along his jawline. 'It's only the size of a cigarette pack. It's clipped into the main-alarm power supply, giving them a two-hour safe period – just the way Manneson said. I'd like to know who made it. And I'd like to know why nobody ever spotted those wires had been cut and retaped.'

'It's a neat job,' mused Moss. 'We took long enough to find it – and we knew where to look. Anyway, anytime it wasn't there the system worked as usual.'

'You left it in position?' asked Ilford quickly, then relaxed as they nodded.

The radio in the corner began murmuring softly. The detective at the handset answered, listened, then came towards them.

'It's on, sir,' he reported happily. 'The security truck's just been taken from the Barbar Agency garage.'

'I'll tell our Mr Daill.' Ilford glanced at his watch. It was seconds after eleven p.m. 'Still no word of Barbar. I'm tempted to phone Doctor Milne, but we'll find out soon enough. Pass the word around, and get those doors relocked. We can have visitors anytime.'

The waiting came hardest now, but at least the bank men had something to do. Urged on by Ilford, watched by the others in a near hypnotized fascination, Daill and his colleagues opened the first package of notes. Counting and checking as they went, they began feeding lots of five hundred pounds into the milling machine. It hummed, it chewed, and tangles of mutilated paper ribbon spouted out at the other end.

The first package was finished and another had been opened when the radio came to life again. Dan Laurence was at the other end and Thane answered.

'Truck's arriving, Colin. Hold on – my fag's gone out.' There was a pause, Thane could hear Laurence's heavy breathing, then he was back on the air. 'Stopped at the door now. We're getting some bonny pictures. Ah – clever laddies. They're in some kind of uniform. And – aye, damn them, nylon-stocking masks. After all the trouble I went to with this camera!'

'Dan' – Thane pressed hard on the send button – 'Dan, how many of them?'

'Six, but one's stayin' with the truck.' Laurence was silent for a moment. 'Front door opening now.' A sharp intake of breath, and a new urgency entered the Bureau chief's voice. 'Colin –'

'Yes?'

'Watch it. If that's not cut-down shotguns some o' them have I'm a gorilla's grannie.'

'Thanks, Dan. Out.' Thane switched off. Every man in the basement was watching him. Only the purr of the incinerator furnace broke the silence.

'Get ready,' he said softly.

The Tallyman's team worked smoothly. Little more than a minute passed before the door at the top of the basement stairway clicked open an inch and stayed that way while the scene below was checked.

It looked innocent enough. Four apparently unsuspecting bank men working busily, stripping wrappings from packages, feeding those ridiculous bundles into the hungry, whining milling machine.

The door opened wide. Crouched low behind the purring furnace, the hot metal roasting against his clothes, Colin Thane watched through a gap between the intake pipes. A burly figure stepped into view, quietly unlocked the top grille, opened it, and came soft-footed down the stairway.

His features were obscured by a nylon-stocking mask. The sawn-off shotgun in his hands was held ready at hip level. And other figures were following.

Thane spared a quick glance in Daill's direction. The banker's round, red face was beaded in sweat. But he worked on, concentrating on his task like his companions.

Four figures were on the stairway, the leader almost at the bottom. Even with that mask, that bull neck and those broad shoulders could only belong to Tank Lewis. But four – Thane cursed, realizing one was still somewhere on top, on guard. Yet the signal had to come from the basement, nowhere else.

He moistened his lips. Lewis had stopped. The grille's manual switch was behind a flapped wall panel on the man's left.

'Now!'

Thane's shout rang and echoed through the basement. The four bank men flopped for the floor, bundles of notes scattering like confetti as they rolled for cover. And, squatting behind a desk, Buddha Ilford began a series of short, piercing blasts on his police whistle.

Fresh sounds of turmoil came from somewhere above on the ground floor. A shotgun sounded its flat boom. Then, unrelated by a couple of seconds, there came a shrill howl of pain. The four startled figures on the stairway jerked to life. One went scrambling back the way they'd come – and the top door slammed shut in his face. Tank Lewis jumped the last few steps, landed in a half-crouch, and swung the shotgun in a wild, searching arc. Behind him, another stocking-masked figure pawed desperately for the flap covering the grille's manual switch.

'We're top and bottom, Lewis – you're the meat in the middle!' Thane hugged the roasting metal as the gun swung. Both barrels blasted. Lead shot hosed a clanging tattoo against the incinerator's front, then Lewis was fumbling to ram fresh shells into the opened breech.

Phil Moss peeped carefully round the edge of the opened safe door, raised his Webley and fired once.

The revolver's sharp, distinctive bark blended with a whining ricochet as the bullet spanged off the stairway wall inches above the manual switch.

That kind of warning didn't need underlining. The man battering against the closed door at the top of the stair turned slowly. The figure by the panel jumped back as if it was poison, and all except Lewis reluctantly raised their hands.

Tank Lewis, the shotgun still opened, took a shambling step forward until his body was pressed against the bars of the grille. He cursed once, followed it with a noise close to a sob, then let the gun fall.

Warily, his Webley trained on the stairway, Buddha Ilford puffed to his feet from behind the desk. As the rest of the basement squad rose from cover he tripped the control switch and the grille rumbled open.

Above them, the top door swung back. A Central Division sergeant looked down, sniffing the cordite-fumed air.

'All right up there?' demanded Ilford.

'Fine, sir.' The sergeant raised a triumphant thumb. 'But the one we grabbed has a helluva sore head.'

'And the driver?'

'Superintendent Laurence has him, sir.'

Satisfied, Ilford waved his free hand. The plain-clothes squad moved in, grabbing the raiders, shoving them with scant ceremony towards the top door.

'Is it over?' Shakily, Patterson Daill came towards them across a carpet of scattered money.

'This part, Mr Daill.' Ilford bent to collect Lewis's shot-gun. 'And thanks for your help. I'll have to talk to the Chief Constable about commendations.'

'That's – ah – that's very kind.' Daill swallowed, automatically straightening his tie. 'Perhaps' – he glanced at Thane with a degree of embarrassment – 'yes, perhaps you were right after all, Chief Inspector. My board believes in any kind of public-spirited action.'

'Nice to know,' grunted Ilford, straight-faced. 'Well, we'll sort this bunch out upstairs. You've a job of your own to finish, eh?'

'Yes.' Daill looked at the scatter of paper and gave a slight shudder. 'I – I wonder if I could have a quick word with Thane?'

'Go ahead,' agreed Ilford. He jerked his head at Phil Moss and they set off together.

Daill cleared his throat awkwardly, conscious that his three colleagues were still hovering in the background. 'Thane, I – ah – I suggest we still have our meeting tomorrow. And I spoke too hastily earlier – well, the situation was unusual.'

'That's how I saw it,' murmured Thane, his face expressionless.

'Anyway, I'll be interested in a further talk.' Daill's manner came a little nearer normal. 'Whatever your decision, I'm sure my Board can be shown that tonight's matter was to everyone's benefit.' Hastily, he added, 'And of course, this talk of a Chief Constable's commendation doesn't enter into my views.'

'Of course not,' said Thane solemnly. He left the banker and went quickly up the stairway.

'Over here, Colin.' Dan Laurence waved an arm across the brightly lit counters, then, grinning, finished rolling himself a fresh cigarette.

The six captives, all handcuffed, were drawn up in a line with their backs to the polished oak of the savings-deposit counter. The last in line was still swaying on his feet, hand clutching his head. Three wore chrome-buttoned tunics which would have passed for uniforms at a rough glance. The rest had dark windcheater jackets and matching slacks. Ilford had already removed two of the nylon masks. The faces beneath were middle-grade hard men – hired help, guessed Thane. Brought in for the job and nothing else.

Ilford dragged another mask away. Blonde hair cascaded down and Janey Milton cursed him in a shrill voice.

'Manners,' protested Ilford.

She spat in his face.

Carefully, Ilford used a handkerchief to wipe himself clean. 'Did you enjoy this morning's hair appointment, Janey?' he asked softly, and drew his own satisfaction from the way her eyes widened. 'Thane, you take the rest.'

Thane's first was Tank Lewis. The coarse, granite face was stubborn, the lips clamped shut. Next in line was Sandy Lang. The ex-con man's beard caught in the fine stocking mesh and he yelped as the nylon was dragged clear. One left now, and it wasn't Barbar – not with that bald head glinting. Thane completed the job, exposed another middle-grade hired help, and stood back with a sigh.

'Thane –' Ilford beckoned and steered him a few paces out of earshot. 'Relax, Colin. We know where he is.'

'We *think* we know,' qualified Thane, his mouth tightening.

'We know,' insisted Ilford. 'Dan got word from Control

170

just as this started. Argyll police found Barbar's car in a ditch a couple of miles past Tyndrum – he'd been trying to squeeze round a snowdrift. They've checked. Barbar walked back to Tyndrum and hired a car and driver. He's at Glen Craig now.'

'Then the sooner I get there the better,' suggested Thane quickly.

'No. He'll keep till we get this lot sorted out.' Ilford turned away and spent almost a minute just looking at the waiting line of prisoners, then spoke in a loud, harsh bark.

'Pay attention. We've had most of you under surveillance, waiting on this caper. We know about Josh Barbar. I'm not particularly interested in what any of you have to say. But some of you are going to be on the wrong end of a murder charge which has nothing to do with this little episode. Any comments?'

No one accepted the invitation.

Ilford shrugged. 'Shovel them out, Sergeant. From here it'll be Central Division, Thane. You don't mind?'

'Saves our laundry bill at Millside,' said Thane unperturbed. 'And while they're being processed Phil and I could take a look over Barbar's apartment.'

'Yes, I think it's time.' Ilford seemed about to add something, then nodded instead. 'Do that. Dan, you'd better go with them.'

Superintendent Laurence yawned and obeyed.

Josh Barbar's home was apartment 4b in a luxury block located near the new Clyde Throughway, the kind of place which had thick carpet in the main hallway.

Glad to be in centrally heated warmth again, Phil Moss located the caretaker, had a brief argument, then returned with the passkey for 4b. They took an elevator up, Dan Laurence muttering under his breath as they stepped out on to more carpet.

Once the door to 4b was opened, Thane led the way and found the light switch.

The flat was small, two rooms plus fitted kitchen and black-tiled bathroom. The furniture ranged from mock antique to leather and chrome, and a white goatskin rug in the middle of the lounge area had a broad cigarette burn near its centre.

'Phil, you bachelors have it made,' sighed Dan Laurence with a touch of regret. 'With a wee bit rearranging this would do me fine.'

Thane smiled fleetingly, thinking of the confusion which constituted Moss's boarding-house room.

They made one slow circuit of the flat in company, then set to work. Laurence settled for the bedroom, Moss took kitchen and bathroom, and Thane started off checking through the lounge.

There is only one way to do a really competent search job, and it amounts to a completely uninhibited attack. Find a drawer, pull it out, turn it upside down. Empty a wardrobe. Roll up a carpet. Take down that picture and examine the back. Take nothing for granted. Be prepared to behave like a vandal – and stifle any thoughts you're in someone's home.

Each knew what he had to do and did it with a swift, remote competence. A resounding clatter and curse from the kitchen told of a stack of tinned food collapsing. Thane's search area gradually narrowed until it came down to a small, ornately carved chest of drawers in one corner of the lounge. It yielded an assortment of oddments, but even with the last of the drawers removed there still seemed something wrong.

He stared at it, moved it around, and was still unsure.

'Now, that's interestin',' declared Dan Laurence, coming up behind him. 'Colin, I haven't seen one o' these since I was in North Africa fighting for King, Country, an' a chance to get on a boat for home. That carving's the giveaway – they're all the same. Made by an Ali Ben somebody or other. Wait now.' He frowned for a moment, then snapped his fingers. 'We'll try this.'

He pressed a section of moulding. There was a click and a shallow drawer inched open.

Laurence grinned. 'I'll get Phil. Looks like we hit the jackpot.'

By the time he returned with Moss, Thane had the drawer removed and the contents spread out.

Two hard-bound notebooks, ruled ledger style and filled with hand-written entries. Three bank books, all issued to different names, all with massive credit balances. A smaller notebook with nothing more than a long list of names, addresses and a few background notes to each.

They'd found The Tallyman's record sheets. How much misery the total represented was something beyond calculation.

'And that just about wraps things up for one Josh Barbar,' said Moss, his eyes gleaming. 'I'm finished, Colin. Nothing to add to the collection.'

'I'd a bit o' luck,' mused Laurence. 'Thane, for a start.' He laid two tiny slips of paper in front of them. 'Underground tickets, issued at St. Enoch station. They were in a suit pocket. What matters maybe more, the same suit's got some wee mud splashes around the trouser legs. And there's more mud on a pair o' shoes. Mud can be damned interesting if you know what to do with it. Particularly if it comes from somewhere around a bus bay. Oh, and I found this – it was on its own, in the back of a drawer.'

He tossed a doorkey down beside the tickets.

Thane nodded slowly and picked it up. 'If this fits Cullen's apartment door –'

'We can check on the way back to Headquarters,' agreed Laurence. 'Let's go. I've got work to do.'

*   *   *

173

The key fitted. Moss made sure of it at a brief stop on the return journey. And at minutes after one a.m., Laurence on his way to the Scientific Bureau's top-floor eyrie, the two Millside detectives were in Buddha Ilford's office.

Ilford listened, examined the collection of ledgers and bank books, and smiled fleetingly.

'Looks like we're not doing too badly all round.' He turned up his rough knuckled hands and surveyed them modestly. 'Mind you, they tried. Take that security truck – they faked the theft down to using jump wires to bypass the ignition. But even if we haven't got anywhere yet with Lewis, Lang or the Milton woman, the hired hands are talking.'

'About Barbar?' queried Moss.

'They've never heard of him – and I believe it,' admitted Ilford sourly. 'But the Alhambra warehouse job is tidied up. They were in on the warehouse raid with Lewis. And your Sergeant MacLeod seems to have picked up the fence they used – plus the bulk of the stuff.'

'He was working on a tip from the docks,' nodded Thane. He switched to the subject which mattered most to him. 'What about Harry Freeman's murder, sir?'

'I'm trying one thing,' said Ilford thoughtfully. 'While you were at Barbar's place I had cars doing the same at the others' homes. They were collecting shoes mainly – but they picked up a pair of horn-rimmed spectacles with plain-glass lenses at Lewis's apartment. Now' – he wagged a forefinger – 'spectacles make a lot of difference to a man's appearance. I've had a pair drawn on a photograph of Lewis and we're trying the result on some of the Fallside bus passengers. Maybe those people won't like being dragged out of bed at this hour, but if we get an identification, plus footprint evidence from Dan and the rest, then Lewis is in as big a sweat as the others.'

Phil Moss gave a sudden, outright laugh. 'The Stafford-shire knot setup – Dan Laurence told me about it in the car,

174

because of that cabinet.' He saw their bewilderment. 'Dan was exiled for a spell in an English regiment, the Stafford-shires. Their cap badge is a three-loop knot – the old sweats' yarn is they had four characters due for hanging and only rope for one. So the fellow who could come up with a knot which would hang the other three at one go was offered . . . was offered . . .' His voice died away under the glum expressions opposite. 'Sorry, sir.'

Ilford grunted. 'If you're finished, let's move to some-thing constructive. This was in Sandy Lang's wallet when he was searched. I've my own idea about what it means.'

He laid a slip of paper on the desk. Scribbled across it were the words 'Glen Craig 16. At two, two ten.'

'That's Doctor Milne's number,' contributed Moss in an attempt to make peace. 'I remember it.'

'Excellent,' said Ilford dryly. 'And the rest?'

Thane hitched himself a little forward in his chair. 'It could be their signal system for tonight,' he said thought-fully. 'Look at it this way – Barbar may have kept his nose clean, but he'll be anxious to know everything went smoothly.'

'So Lang calls him at that hour?' Ilford deliberately put the obvious, shaking his head.

'No,' agreed Thane. 'He couldn't speak to him – not without waking the whole household. But – but suppose he called the number, hung up as soon as someone answered, then called again and did the same. Barbar would hear the phone ringing each time. It would be enough.'

'That's how I see it,' murmured Ilford. He glanced at his watch. 'Forty minutes before the first call is due. And I want the Scientific Bureau reports before I do more.' He relaxed a little. 'Well, the switchboard usually have a kettle boiling about now.'

The switchboard had, and the Headquarters brand of tea

was strong brew. After two cups, Moss fell back on his reserve of bismuth tablets, glad that the clock showed it was time for the first call.

Thane passed the number. The line rang out with the slow, erratic beat of a country automatic exchange. At last: there was a click.

'Glen Craig 16 –' Milne's voice was sleepy but distinct.

Thane hung up.

Dan Laurence entered the room ten minutes later, as he was repeating the performance. This time the receiver at the other end was lifted more quickly. Milne's voice was irate.

Thane hung up again, grinning a little.

'Party games?' queried Laurence, puzzled.

'Investigative procedure,' parried Ilford dryly. 'Beneath a technical expert's understanding, Dan. Well, any luck?'

'Aye.' Laurence pushed aside some files on the desk and perched himself on the cleared space. 'Lewis, the Milton woman and Barbar are the three who were out at Fallside. We've matched shoeprint patterns and traces of mud. They're as good as fingerprints in evidence. The mud from Barbar's trousers also matches against local samples. I'll bet my shirt we get the same result on activation analysis, an' that's foolproof.' He glanced at Thane. 'I mean it, Colin. We can pin that mud down to within a matter of yards usin' nuclear radiation.'

The telephone rang and Ilford answered it. The conversation was brief and he hung up with a faint smile. 'Confirmation, Dan. We've two identifications from bus passengers who've seen that photograph showing Lewis wearing glasses.'

'I told you.' The Bureau chief slid down from the desk, satisfied. 'Well, I'm away to my bed before anyone else knows I'm around.'

They let him go. Ilford went into his contemplation pose and Thane waited, exchanging a brief, silent shrug with

176

Moss. There was no sense in trying to push the pace with Ilford. The C.I.D. chief set his own speed, particularly in his own territory.

At last, Ilford stirred. Reaching out, he flipped the desk intercom.

'Lang, Lewis, Milton – bring them through,' he ordered.

It didn't take long. The trio arrived escorted by two Central detectives and a uniformed w.p.c. Lewis still wore handcuffs.

'Leave them,' snapped Ilford.

The escorts departed. As the door closed, Ilford glared sourly at the prisoners. Janey Milton was in the middle, her blonde hair tousled, her mouth a tight, cynical line. On her left, Tank Lewis stood in the typical Glasgow 'hard man' pose – shoulders hunched, feet apart, the faint sneer on his face a carbon copy of a thousand others. Only Sandy Lang seemed uneasy. The bearded mouth twitched a little, his bright eyes darting around the room.

'Looking for Barbar?' asked Ilford heavily. 'Don't worry about him, Lang. He's probably tucked up comfortably in bed. We made those two calls for you – didn't want to disappoint him.'

Lang gnawed his lip, but said nothing.

Ilford sighed and opened one of the files on his desk. 'Well, where do we start with you? Last night, Lang, when you gave Detective Inspector Moss a light for his cigarette?'

Moss chuckled. Lang jerked round, wide-eyed recognition ending in a groan.

'Or you, Janey? Tank shouldn't have given you that transistor set. It was too hot. But maybe he needed his money till he reached the betting shop this morning.' He glanced at Lewis. 'Second favourite in the two-thirty came up, but the rest are still running, right?'

Lewis flexed his shoulders and the 'cuff links clinked.

'Helluva clever,' he said conversationally to Janey Milton. 'Do you think they grow cops somewhere, or put them together in a factory?'

She wasn't amused. 'You and your damned radio!'

'Aye.' His nose wrinkled. 'Ach, well, it happened.'

'It hardly matters now, Janey,' said Thane softly. He pointed to their feet. All three were wearing canvas shoes, cells issue. 'Find them comfortable enough?' He glanced at Ilford, received a nod, and went on. 'We'll need your shoes till after the trial. They say that Janey and Tank were out at Fallside, that they helped murder Harry Freeman.'

Lang swallowed hard. 'But not me, Chief Inspector. I wasn't there. You had me followed – so you know it.'

'Shut up,' said Lewis savagely, speaking barely above a whisper out of a dry mouth. 'Stay quiet, damn you.'

Phil Moss shoved his hands deep in his pockets, balanced back until his chair was teetering, and belched gently. 'Then there was Cullen,' he reminded cheerfully. 'He didn't last long once we let him go. Your Tallyman's got some unpleasant habits. But you know one thing that helped us a lot?' He dropped his voice to a confidential level. 'That Alhambra warehouse job. Being greedy – pulling that just before the big one was a big mistake.'

'And we know who's to blame for that,' spat Janey Milton. 'He was told the warehouse job was off, but – but –' She turned, swung her clenched fist, and hit Lewis hard on the mouth.

She was swinging again when Thane dragged her back. Blood trickling from a cut lip, Lewis grimaced.

'Ach, Janey –'

'If anyone feels like talking privately to us, we'll arrange it,' murmured Ilford. 'What about you, Janey?'

'Me?' She sniffed. 'Mister, you know what you can do for a start.'

'Lang?'

The onetime confidence trickster hesitated, then shook his head. 'I just didn't kill anyone, that's all.'

'And no sense in asking you, Lewis,' said Ilford resignedly.

Tank Lewis brought his handcuffed wrists up to his mouth and wiped the blood clear. His ugly face went through a minor contortion of emotions.

'Janey an' me were goin' to get hitched once,' he said suddenly and unexpectedly.

'An ideal match,' murmured Ilford. 'So?'

'So – ach, so you've got Barbar anyway, right? An' there's no sense in either o' us letting him get in first with his story.'

Lewis avoided looking at any of them. 'He did for Freeman. We were there, but it was him that pulled that fancy throat-poke bit. An' he hinted he'd had to fix Cullen because the Millside bunch were too interested.'

Janey Milton stared at him, bemused, then sighed. 'Tank, you great, bloody fool!'

He shuffled his feet, embarrassed, his face scarlet.

'You'll make a statement?' asked Thane sharply.

'Aye.'

'Take them out,' said Ilford, a quiver of disbelief still in his voice. 'Get Lewis's statement. And give the other two a chance after that to – to change their minds if they want.'

Moss led the way. As Thane made to take up the rear of the procession, Buddha Ilford spoke again.

'Stay a minute, Colin – just you.'

Thane glanced back, holding the door open with his foot.

'Close it. Come back here and sit down.'

He did. Eyeing him strangely, Ilford opened a drawer, took out a dusty hundred box of cigarettes, and offered them. Thane took one and lit it. The tobacco was dry and he wondered just who'd given the box to Ilford and when.

'Thanks.' He drew on the smoke, waiting.

Ilford shifted a little in his chair, then opened his lips in an odd, clench-toothed grimace which might have been meant as a smile. 'This is none of my damned business, Colin. But I talked to Patterson Daill while we were waiting in that basement.'

'Yes, sir?' Thane felt a chill beginning somewhere roughly halfway down between his shoulder blades.

'It – ah' – Ilford ran a fingertip lightly along his collar – 'he let it slip that the bank has made you an offer. I don't know the details. I didn't ask and I don't want to know. I just felt that' – he stopped and shrugged – 'well, good divisional officers don't grow on trees. Made up your mind yet?'

'I thought I had.' Thane gave a lopsided grin across the desk. 'But I've changed it since – several times.'

'It's *your* choice.' Ilford pursed his lips, frowning down. 'In your shoes – well, dammit, I'm not in them, so that doesn't matter. I started off as a cop back in the depression days when there was nothing else except the dole queues. The nearest I've had to offers of alternative employment since is when my wife wants me to dry the dishes. But look at all the angles first. Be very sure, Colin. That's my advice.'

Thane was the one who now felt uncomfortable. 'I will. And I was planning to tell you the moment anything was agreed, sir.'

'That's still time enough. Just don't let them rush you into a decision.' Ilford shoved his chair back with a mumble of relief. 'Right, let's see how Moss is getting on.'

It was one thing for Tank Lewis to be willing to tell his story, another altogether to get it on paper. The two words 'voluntary statement' make any Scottish policeman shudder. Each step of the way has its own rigid procedure laid

180

down by law. Mishandle just one step and the 'voluntary statement' will be thrown out of court before a jury catches even a scent of its existence.

The interview-room clock had passed four a.m. before Lewis's story was complete and he'd signed each page of the typed verbatim copies. In another office along the same corridor Janey Milton had just announced she wanted to do the same. Only Lang still held out.

'Wrong again,' admitted Ilford as Lewis was taken from the smoke-filled room on his way to the cells. 'I'd have backed Lang as the one who'd crumble first.'

Thane nodded. Over by the table, Phil Moss sorted the last of the statement sheets into order, then yawned and stretched. His own eyes felt heavy.

'There's still Barbar,' he reminded pointedly. 'I'd like to be at Glen Craig before he's too wide-awake.'

Ilford rasped a hand along his chin, then grunted agreement. 'We can handle the woman without you. Get on your way soon as you're ready.'

Moss made a noise like a groan. For a moment he almost envied Tank Lewis, tucked up in a cell with a spring mattress and the regulation issue of blankets.

Five minutes later they were on their way in one of the night-shift Headquarters cars, the driver a hatchet-faced taciturn individual who chewed gum and said little.

The city and suburbs gave way to snow-covered fields and the first hills. As the car ate its way on through the night, Thane let his eyelids droop. Beside him, Moss was already asleep, mouth open, making gentle snoring noises. Just Glen Craig now. Then it would be over . . .

When he woke it was still dark but the car had stopped and another car was drawn up ahead. He nudged Moss back to consciousness and leaned forward.

'Where are we?'

'Just over the Argyll County border, sir,' said the driver. 'Looks like a welcoming committee.'

A uniformed inspector came towards them. Thane opened his door and stepped out, shivering in the cold predawn air. The snow underfoot was sugar-crisp.

'Good morning.' The Argyll man sounded indecently bright and cheerful. 'Chief Inspector Thane? The name's MacFarran. How was the trip?'

'I wouldn't know.' Thane glanced at his watch. The luminous hands showed a quarter past six. 'Ask our driver – he was awake.'

MacFarran gave a sympathetic chuckle. 'Well, I've got three men in the car. Glen Craig's about fifteen minutes on. But – ah – of course, you know the road.'

'I walked part of it last time,' agreed Thane wryly.

'I know. I helped with your car. We dumped it in a garage at Tyndrum.' MacFarran made it clear that 'dumping' seemed the most appropriate word. 'Well, we'll lead on to the house if you want. It's your show after that.'

A minute later, the county car's taillights their guide, they were under way again. The Headquarters driver surprisingly produced a flask of coffee which was still steaming hot, hot enough to scald the two Millside men fully awake while the two-car convoy made a fast job of covering the final stretch.

Grumbling to himself, Moss peered out at what he could see of the white wilderness. 'Is that the place?' Unexpectedly, he pointed ahead.

Yes.' Thane frowned as he spoke. The house lay about a quarter mile on, lights burning behind some of the windows. Perturbed, he sat gnawing his lip as the gap closed, then had his door open almost before they stopped. He got out quickly and looked around. Despite the lights there was no sign of life.

'They're early risers,' mused Moss, joining him. Mac-Farran arrived a second later, leaving his men in the car.

They went to the house door, rang the bell, and waited. It opened after a few moments. The woman who looked out was middle-aged, plump, and wore a wrap-round apron.

'It's yourself, Archie MacFarran!' The Highland accent was strong, and she smiled as she recognized the Argyll man.

'Bright and early,' agreed MacFarran. He glanced at Thane. 'This is Jenny, Doctor Milne's housekeeper.'

'Aye, and if it is the doctor you're looking for you've missed him,' she said bluntly. 'They've not long left. Breakfast before six, and away off up the glen to join this deer stalk.'

'All of them?' demanded Thane. 'Including Barbar?'

'That one too.' She saw the two cars and frowned. 'What's the fuss about?'

'Later, Jenny,' said MacFarran swiftly. 'Where's the starting point?'

'Up by the Eagle Loch.'

Thane swore softly. 'Milne said an early start – but I didn't think he meant this early!'

'That's the way up here. Rendezvous ready to head off at first light,' explained MacFarran quickly. 'If Barbar gets off on foot into those hills, and with a gun –'

'Then we've a real job,' finished Thane grimly. 'Let's go.'

Milne's housekeeper was still shaking her head in the doorway when the cars roared off.

The road to Eagle Loch was narrow, rutted, and badly drifted in places. But the Argyll car set a fast pace, and behind it Thane's driver dropped his silence in favour of a cursing commentary as he strove to keep up.

And time was creeping round. Dawn was a pink line staining the white horizon of hills when the Argyll car suddenly slowed to little more than a crawl. Then its lights went out. They did the same, rounded another corner, and realized why.

A few hundred yards ahead about a dozen vehicles were

183

parked along the roadside. Most were go-anywhere Land-Rovers, and they could see groups of people moving around them.

The two cars coasted part of the distance, then stopped. As he got out, Thane saw that the gathering ahead was just beside a small hill which had a grey outcrop of rock shaped like an eagle's outthrust beak. And so far their arrival seemed unnoticed.

MacFarran had his men out and waiting.

'Any way you want it,' he said softly.

Thane nodded. 'Then Phil and I go in first. Stay spread out and ready for trouble – but hang back unless it happens. If he sees a uniform too soon, he's liable to bolt.'

MacFarran didn't argue.

Quietly, Moss by his side, Colin Thane walked quickly over the snow. As they reached the fringe of the shooting party he reckoned there were about thirty, a few of them women, most of the men in thick tweeds and carrying rifles. They passed the first few, drew some curious glances, but kept on.

He saw Doctor Milne a moment later. The heart specialist was standing on his own, hands in his pockets.

He nudged Moss and they veered towards the man.

'Doctor –'

Milne turned, frowned in the grey light, then his mouth framed a silent exclamation.

'Where is he?' asked Thane quietly.

'So it's like that?' Milne drew a deep breath. 'He's with my daughter. We've the last Land-Rover in the line and –' Suddenly, looking past them, his eyes widened.

Thane spun round. Josh Barbar and the girl had been coming towards them. They were less than a dozen yards away.

Barbar stared at him. The thin, white face twisted in a spasm of fear, recognition and understanding. Then he acted. Just to his right a couple were unloading equipment from a station wagon. A rifle was propped against the opened door.

He went for it in a clawing dive, scooped it up, and in a single movement jacked a cartridge from the magazine into the breech.

For another instant the rifle said all that was necessary. Barbar backed a few paces, the rifle held chest-high, its muzzle training first on Thane, then suddenly switching to Helen Milne.

'I'm leaving,' he said hoarsely. 'Nobody tries to stop me. Understand?'

No one spoke, no one moved. Out on the fringe, beyond the vehicles, Thane caught a glimpse of uniforms. He said a quick, silent prayer the county men would realize the situation.

'There are plenty of rifles here, Barbar,' he said suddenly. 'These people came to hunt deer. But that could change.'

Barbar laughed, a strange, half-strangled sound. 'But I'd make a hell of a poor hatstand, remember? And maybe they wouldn't be so brave if what they were hunting was liable to shoot back.'

The county men had stopped. All around, people were gradually moving clear. Out of the corner of his eye Thane saw a man in a leather jacket begin reaching slowly towards his rifle. Then MacFarran appeared at the man's side, gripping his wrist, silently shaking his head.

'I want the keys of the Land-Rover, Doctor,' said Barbar sharply. 'Throw them over here, on the ground.'

Milne hesitated then, as Thane nodded, brought the keys from his pocket and tossed them over.

'Helen ' – the rifle swung a fraction – 'pick them up. Now.'

Tight-lipped, she shook her head.

'Do it.' His voice became a snarl. 'Then we're going to back up to the Land-Rover together, and nobody's going to move.'

Milne groaned and took a half-step forward. 'Barbar –'

The muzzle came back again. But the girl suddenly bent down and picked up the keys. She rose slowly, watching him.

'That's better.' A touch of his old confidence insinuated into Barbar's manner. 'When we get there, you drive.'

She nodded, turning. He moved to follow her, stepping backwards; keeping them all in his vision. Thane had his right hand in his coat pocket, firmly round the Webley's butt, his finger on the trigger. Yet the chance of a shot under these conditions was ludicrously slim. He could only wait.

Then it happened, very, very simply. Helen Milne seemed to stumble, dropped the keys, and bent as if to pick them up again. Her hand went down – then scooped hard and fast. The keys and a handful of wet, blinding snow flew through the air and hit Barbar in the face, the snow coating against his spectacles. And she threw herself desperately towards the shelter of the nearest car.

Barbar jerked and fired blindly. The bullet smashed against the car and whined off into the dawn – but the girl was clear. He wiped a frantic sleeve across the spectacle lenses, jacked another cartridge into the breech, and swung the weapon in search of a target. He swung again, then stopped, bewildered.

No signal had been given. But police and hunting party alike had melted back into cover.

Lying flat behind a station wagon's front wheel, the Webley out, Colin Thane heard rifle bolts click here and there in the greying dawn. Quickly, he levered himself up on one elbow.

'Police,' he bellowed. 'Leave him to us. Barbar –'

The rifle swung, spat, and the station wagon's windshield shattered. Thane rolled out from the edge of the wheel, left hand gripping right wrist, and fired once.

The .38 bullet hit Barbar high on the left shoulder,

knocking him almost off balance. He gave an animal-like yelp, dropped the rifle, and clasped his shoulder.

Thane rose from cover. Barbar saw him, started to stoop for the rifle again, and a gun blasted from somewhere further along the line of vehicles. The bullet spouted snow upwards just at his feet. The warning was enough. Barbar spun round and began to run, away from the road, out into the snow-covered moorland.

Milne had his daughter in his arms. The man in the leather jacket reappeared, rifle cradled at the ready. It was a heavy .38 with telescopic sights.

'Want him?' asked the man hopefully.

'Not that way.' Thane broke into a run over the ankle-deep snow, Phil Moss already scrambling in pursuit a few yards ahead.

Voices shouted from the roadside and other figures were running. He overtook Moss, saw Barbar now about a hundred yards ahead, and then the man stopped, his right hand coming up, something in it.

Instinctively, Thane swerved. He heard a click in the cold, clear air, then another. Despairing, Barbar threw the automatic aside and began running again.

The shouts from the roadside grew faint yet somehow more urgent. Thane ignored them. Ahead, Barbar reached a flat, level stretch which appeared firmer going and picked up speed immediately. Floundering on, Thane gathered himself for a fresh effort – and was suddenly tackled hard round the knees.

He crashed down. It was MacFarran who had tackled him, and the Argyll inspector held on firmly when he tried to rise.

'Don't be a damned fool, man,' said MacFarran urgently, breath steaming, rank and everything else forgotten. 'Didn't you hear us shouting?'

Thane shook his head. Moss was coming towards them

at a slow trot, a few others were strung out further behind.

'I stopped Moss, but this was the only way to get you,' said MacFarran grimly, releasing his grip. 'Watch Barbar if you want. But that's Eagle Loch he's on. It froze over just before the snow and there's damned near bottomless water underneath. We can't stop him now – I'd a bad enough time with you.'

Thane scrambled to his feet. 'You mean the ice –'

'Won't bear him once he gets any distance out. That's always the way with Eagle Loch.'

Moss reached them. Side by side they watched the running man. Ahead of Barbar the sun had begun to lip the horizon and the pale-pink hills were shading to a deep red. They could see now how that flat, platelike surface of ice and its thin crusting of snow stretched for an area of half a mile before the opposite bank began.

They could tell the exact moment when Josh Barbar finally realized his danger. He staggered to a halt, looked back, changing direction, slipped and almost fell, then took a few more steps.

At that distance there was no sound as the surface broke. They saw a large section of ice cant upwards like some stiff, ragged-edged sail. As it settled again, Barbar had gone and they could hear screaming.

'We've got to try,' said Thane grimly.

'Aye,' admitted MacFarran. 'But careful we don't join him.'

Spaced apart, they set off at a jog trot with the ice soon groaning beneath their feet. Now they could see Barbar, his head a pale blob in a patch of dark water. Legs splashing, he reached the edge of the broken ice, clung, and tried to pull himself up. The ice disintegrated and he fell back again.

He saw them coming.

'Thane' – the name came in a voice high with terror – 'Thane, help me. Please.'

Two steps on, Colin Thane heard a loud, grating sound, and a jagged crack ran quickly from where he stood to the edge of that freezing water.

'She won't bear,' yelled MacFarran from his right. 'Moss, watch it –'

Thane glanced round. Phil Moss's right foot had gone through and the wiry figure lurched forward, then performed a brief miracle of balance in dragging clear. Moss didn't go on, and no one could have blamed him.

Thane looked ahead. Barbar was staring at him, no longer splashing, fingertips fastened like claws to the ice, mouth shaping an unspoken appeal.

Another step forward and the groaning ice gave a sickening sway. He had to spread his weight, and quickly. Dropping on hands and knees, breathing heavily, Thane tried to inch forward.

'Thane –' The voice choked and ended.

Colin Thane could see only a slight swirl on the surface of the black, suddenly empty water. The Tallyman had gone. He waited, but there were no bubbles, no signs that Josh Barbar had ever existed.

Trembling in a way which had nothing to do with the temperature, he started back.

MacFarran and Moss were waiting where the ice was firm. Moss held out his left hand, a Beretta automatic lying flat along the palm.

'I picked it up back there,' he said soberly. 'It's loaded, but – well, I know why it didn't work.'

'Cullen's?' asked Thane.

Moss nodded. 'I told you I fixed the firing pin. Barbar wouldn't know until he pulled the trigger.' He looked back towards the loch. 'What happens now?'

'That's *my* problem,' mused Inspector MacFarran. The county man produced his cigarettes, passed them round, and struck a match. He lit his own last and drew on it between cupped fingers. 'Ach, we'll find him in the spring. I'm damned if I'm letting anyone else risk his neck.' He glanced pointedly at Thane. 'As it is, we're lucky he's the only one under there . . .'

Thane shrugged, knowing the man was right yet remembering that look on Barbar's face.

'Ach, who the hell would be a cop?' sighed MacFarran. 'I suppose somebody's always got to be around – maybe that's what it's all about. I don't know.'

Figures were crossing the snow towards them. Still shaking his head, he went in their direction. The two Millside men stood silent for a moment, each with his own thoughts.

Moss shivered. 'Let's get back to somewhere warm before I catch pneumonia,' he said suddenly. 'And you've that appointment at the bank. Lord knows how you'll make it in time.'

'I'm not going,' said Thane quietly. 'Forget it, Phil.'

It was no good. He was a cop, and he was stuck with the fact.

He wondered how Mary would feel. But it would work out, that much he did know.

Maybe he'd have time to look at his car on the way back. Then he'd have to see Ilford. There was a matter of a week's leave overdue. If he really put the screws on Headquarters, he could take it now. Mary's mother was always eager for a chance to look after the kids.

A few days by the sea somewhere.

He owed Mary that much, for a start.

A faint grin crossed his face and he tossed the cigarette aside.

'Ready?' asked Moss hopefully.

He nodded, and they started back towards the cars.